QUARAN
IN THE GRAND HOTEL

QUARANTINE IN THE GRAND HOTEL

by

Jenő Rejtő

CORVINA

Published in Hungary 2005
by Corvina Books Ltd.
1072 Budapest
Rákóczi út 16. Hungary

Translated from
Vesztegzár a Grand Hotelban
by Jenő Rejtő

Copyright © Heirs of Jenő Rejtő
English translation © István Farkas

On the cover: János Vaszary, City Lights, 1930

ISBN 963 13 5374 5

Printed in Hungary

1.

When Maud returned to her room, she saw a man emerge from her wardrobe. Dressed in pyjamas and wearing a smart green lampshade on his head, the stranger beamed a friendly smile at her.

"Excuse me," he said, politely raising the lampshade. "My name is Felix Van der Gullen."

Having recovered from her shock, Maud backed towards the door. The stranger must clearly be mad.

"What are you doing here," she inquired of the intruder. "What business had you in my wardrobe?"

"Please don't shout," said the lunatic stranger. "If you do you'll bring about the downfall of a good-natured, cheerful fellow, who is about to leave these premises anyway."

"What were you doing in my wardrobe," Maud said once again, demanding a clear answer.

"I – I just happened to walk into it."

"How did you get into my room?"

"Oh, I entered through the window early this morning. You see, I happened to be on the run, and out there, in the deserted garden of the hotel, I spotted this open window. So I hoisted myself onto the windowsill, and peeked in. Seeing that the bed was unoccupied, I hopped in and hid in the wardrobe. I was nervous and excited, you see, so in that flustered state I... well, I fell into a deep sleep... I woke up just a moment ago. While in there, I seem to have torn the loop of a sports jacket. I apologize."

As Maud made no reply, the stranger removed the lampshade that had fallen onto his head in the wardrobe, and placed it gingerly on the table. He made a bow and started for the door.

"Stop right there," Maud cried.

"As you wish," said the mad stranger, halting in his track.

"Are you out of your mind? What do you mean leaving my room clad in pyjamas?"

The stranger submissively made for the window.

"No," Maud cried out at a high pitch that just stopped short of a scream.

"Right-o."

Startled, the stranger stepped back and froze in the attitude of one prepared to obey any order that might come his way.

Maud peered down into the garden in despair. It was rapidly filling up with arriving guests.

"If a man in pyjamas climbed out of my room into that garden, my reputation would be ruined for good."

"That might put a complexion on the situation that would certainly be embarrassing," the stranger conceded. "However, afterwards, you could, perhaps... er... call the guests aside... and er... I mean, one by one... and explain to them who the person was they had seen climbing out of here..."

"Easier said than done. I'm in the dark about that myself."

"True enough," Felix Van der Gullen nodded sadly. "So, under the present circumstances, it looks like I'm going to have to stay," he announced as he made himself comfortable in an armchair. "You haven't got a cigarette by any chance?"

"What do you think you're doing, staying in my room dressed like that?"

The stranger slapped his thigh in exasperation. "I beg your pardon, Miss..."

"Borckman," Maud said mechanically.

"I beg your pardon, Miss Borckman!" Realizing a fleeting advantage in his situation, the stranger was speaking with less reserve now. "If I am not to leave this room either through the door or through the window, then, evidently, I am constrained to stay here. You can't expect a man, even in a position and a state in which I happen to find myself, to vanish into thin air. Or go into regress and disappear like an appendicitis attack. Surely, you can't mean that!"

Maud was nonplussed. "Well, something *ought* to be done about this," she said. "There must be a way."

"Now, Miss Borckman, I am aware of your situation, and I fully sympathize with you in your quandary. Indeed, people are inclined to put a wrong interpretation on the sudden appearance of a man in pyjamas."

"Shame on you!"

"*Honi soit qui mal y pense*. I say, do you really grudge me a smoke?"

Maude picked up a box of cigarettes from a small table by the side of the bed, and flung it to him. He cheerfully extracted one, lit up, then pocketed the box.

"Silly business, this," he declared, comfortably leaning back in his chair.

"I still do not know who you are," Maud said angrily. "I can't decide whether you are a criminal or a lunatic. But whichever is the case, I ought to put a bullet through you, just for getting me into this dreadful spot."

"That *would* get you out of this fix," the stranger said, "though the solution seems entirely too drastic to me. Look, if you think that by doing so I can save your good repute and make amends for what I've done, I shall be only too glad to marry you," he offered politely. "That would be a good sight better than being shot at and killed, though obviously, not all my friends would agree with me on that."

"Look, Mr. Van der Gullen," Maud said, "I am going to check out this evening. I want you to stay in this room until then and, if possible, leave only in the dead of night. Understand? I should also warn you that once I make up my mind, I don't care about my reputation. One wrong move, and I shall turn you over to the hotel detective."

"Yes, that would be just like you," the stranger nodded as if he and Maud were old friends. " I will do my best to get into your good graces."

"You won't get the chance," Maude countered, "I'm locking you up in the bathroom right now, and I won't be letting you out until I leave the hotel tonight."

The stranger looked pained. "You wouldn't have the heart to take an unfair advantage of the situation of a defenceless man," he hazarded plaintively.

"I'm going to do just that. Take your choice: it's either the wardrobe or the bathroom."

"You going to lock me up?... Think it over. Reflect. Consider the facts. Taking an unprotected man prisoner and holding him captive…"

"If you take such a frivolous attitude, you may come off worse still."

"You're not planning to flog me?" he said in mock alarm. Though she was very angry, Maud couldn't help laughing.

"I've a good mind to turn you over to the police. What you've done calls for punishment. And it ought to be a stiff one," she went on, still more angrily. "You seem to have absolutely no regrets for having got a respectable lady into such a fix. And in a first class hotel to boot!"

"How do you know my position isn't a hundred times worse than yours? You've no idea how badly I am suffering right this minute."

Slightly concerned, she made an unintentional step towards him,.

"Is anything the matter with you?"

"Yes. I may die of starvation any moment." He then added in a sepulchral voice: "It is noon, and I haven't had lunch yet."

"Well, I never... I shouldn't be surprised if you turned out to be a robber with a warrant out for your arrest. I've never seen a person displaying so much cynicism..."

"Look, my dear tyrant. Before I start serving my term in the bathroom, let me tell you that *your* conduct leaves much to be desired as well."

"I beg your pardon. Just what *do* you mean by that?"

"You rebuke me for having unfairly dragged your name through the mud in the eyes of society. On the other hand... come to think of it..." His voice sounded grim, even accusatory. "Where, may I ask, were you tonight?"

"What?"

"You heard me. Why did I clamber into this room, of all the rooms in this hotel? Because it was empty. And why was it empty? Because you were not in it. Had you been in this bed, asleep, I would have discreetly removed myself from the windowsill, and should not now be facing the threat of captivity in the bathroom where, in order to avoid death by starvation, I'll be compelled to eat a bar of soap... Yes, Miss Borckman." And at this juncture he raised his voice like a stern prosecutor speaking at a criminal trial. "Where *were* you between four and five o'clock this morning?"

Maud was flabbergasted. She was overwhelmed by the stupendous impertinence of the pyjama-clad stranger. After a while, she broke the silence.

"I'm not going to lock you up in the bathroom, after all."

"Is it the wardrobe, then?"

"No. I'm going to turn you over to the hotel detective."

"All right," the stranger said sadly. "If you must." He sighed deeply, and made for the door, like a man about to mount the scaffold.

"Wait!" Maud cried, stamping a foot in anger. "Good heavens, what a frightful mess!... Stay right where you are!"

"I won't. No. You insulted me."

She clutched at his arm. "I was joking. You must not be seen emerging from my room, dressed in your pyjamas."

He heaved a sigh and, looking heroic and grim, shook his head.

"I should give myself up to the detective, after all. You were right A man like me must not be allowed to go unpunished." In a tragic gesture he twice beat his chest. "I want to get the punishment I deserve," he exclaimed.

Maud grabbed his arm.

"For heaven' sake, don't shout!" she implored him.

"I won't have you lock me up in a bathroom!" the stranger countered.

"I am not going to lock you up," Maud said softly, her resolve broken.

"Ah, that alters the matter," the stranger said. "In that case, just possibly, I'll stay." He sat down again. "I'm actually not a bad chap when a lady needs my help. I can always be counted on to rescue a damsel in distress."

At this moment there came a knock on the door.

2.

Tense silence descended on the room.

At last Muad spoke. "Who is it?" she asked in an unsteady voice.

"Prince Sergius."

She turned, intending to tell the intruder that he should go to the bathroom, but the insolent stranger was nowhere to be seen. The knocking was repeated, this time somewhat impatiently.

"Just a moment," Maud replied in a tone of feigned liveliness. "I'm just finishing getting dressed." Presently, she called out in a cheerful tone: "Come in."

As the door opened she adjusted her dress, pretending to apply the finishing touches for the benefit of the man who was entering.

The Prince was a man getting on sixty, lean, white-haired with fine features and a pair of strikingly clear blue eyes radiating intelligence in a pale face.

"You weren't down for lunch, Maud. Why?"

"I tore a clasp from my dress as I was putting it on. It's all right now. We can go," she added quickly.

"Aha!" thought the cheeky stranger, who was now hiding under the bed. "She is anxious to see the bounder out of the room. She seems to be loath to let me hear what they're going to talk about. I ought to stop my ears, I suppose. But I'm not going to do so. Shame on me!"

These are the thoughts that were crossing the impertinent stranger's mind under the bed as he was trying to fight off his craving for a smoke.

The Prince was playing for time. "Just a few words," he said. "We shan't be by ourselves at lunch. Did you speak with him?"

Maud dug her heels in. "We will talk about that later," she said.

"No. I must know everything if I am to accept this sacrifice. They'll send you to jail, and as for me…"

"Stop! Please."

"But we're by ourselves here, aren't we?"

"Yes. Yes. But suppose someone should happen to be eavesdropping."

Well, well, the cheeky stranger thought. So this very attractive and very respectable young lady is facing a chance of incarceration. Well, well!

The old man lowered his voice.

"What did you tell him?"

"Let's go, please, and have lunch. And not another word about this matter."

"You're all nerves, my dear. I thought you were a strong young lady".

"There's nothing wrong with my nerves. It's just that… This is one of my off-days. So let's just go." She was on the verge of tears.

"Just one thing more. At eight o'clock this evening a three-engine plane will fly you to Singapore, and the police…"

"Let us go!… Now!"

"But I…"

"Ask no questions. Please! Off we go!"

A pretty kettle of fish, thought the insolent stranger. And *she* wanted to lock *me* up in the bathroom!

"All right, Maud. Let's go." The Prince offered her his arm. She heaved a sigh of relief as she made to go. But just then, a knock came at the door.

"Who is it?" Maud asked

"The police," a harsh voice boomed out.

3.

Silence.

Slowly, the white-haired man's hand began creeping towards his hip-pocket. Maud seized his arm with both hands before he could grab his gun. Then, the very opposite of the nervous, worried woman she had been but a moment ago, calmly, almost matter-of-factly, she called out:

"Do you mean you want to see *me*? What kind of a silly joke is this?"

"The police request all the guests staying in this hotel to please come down to the foyer."

"What on earth for?"

"The Grand Hotel is under quarantine," replied the voice. Footsteps could be heard receding, and presently there was knocking on the door of the adjacent room..

"We're done for," said the Prince after a moment's silence.

"Nonsense. And you'd better stop snatching at your hip pocket"

"Making that movement reassures me. As long as I've got a gun on me..."

"I don't want you to say things like that," Maud snapped.

Now there's another one she's going to lock up in the bathroom, thought the frivolous stranger under the bed.

"First of all, we will now go down to the foyer and find out what's going on in this hotel."

"But if you fail to get away from this place tonight, all will have been lost!"

"Until we see for ourselves what's going on here, we can't know that."

The young man heard the door being shut, and sighed a sigh of relief. He waited for a few seconds, then decided to crawl out from under the bed.

He heard a rustle.

The noise made him crawl back quickly. Now what was *this*? Slowly, the door was opened, and the floor creaked under some footsteps. Someone coming to do the room, maybe? Not likely. Whoever was entering was doing so with much caution. *Sneaking* in, he or she was, he would call it.

He was itching to take a peek, but all he could see was a pair of feet. White tennis shoes, somewhat smudgy. The cap of one of them bore an odd-shaped brown stain. Probably from coffee.

The sneakers were leaving. The door was shut.

He saw his change.

Quickly, he crawled out from under the bed. If the guests were down in the lobby, then the garden must be deserted, he reckoned. He looked round the room, and spotted a letter on the table. Look at that! That was what the wearer of those white tennis shoes with one of them marked by that odd-shaped coffee stain had sneaked in with.

The typewritten address on the letter said:

"For Miss Borckman, First floor, Room No. 72."

Never mind that. Get on, he urged himself.

He sidled up to the window, but immediately recoiled from what it saw.

What on earth is going on here? he asked himself. Had this hotel become a theatre of war?

In the garden below, a detachment of sappers was busy putting up a barbed wire fence. Clearly, they had just started working a short while ago, but already the bristling barrier was in position, surrounding the garden in a semicircle, and sentries with fixed bayonets had been posted along the far side of it. Stacked rifles, a steaming large, deep pot, and troops bivouacked were in view. The army had occupied the area surrounding the hotel.

The impertinent stranger stood by the window, puzzled. Then he hung his head and, turning, retired to the bathroom, and voluntary captivity.

4.

Three years previously, Little Lagonda, one of the Bali group of islands near the south-eastern tip of Java, had been living in primordial obscurity. As a matter of fact it was Lund Wolfgang, the celebrated painter, who had triggered the economic boom on the modest little island by churning out picture after picture in Surabaya and who, more recently, sold fewer and fewer of his masterpieces. Things had been different when his wife was still alive. Daughter of a sugar manufacturer, she was a refined, sophisticated person, attractive and pleasant, but exceedingly squint-eyed. However, it wasn't outward appearance the painter was after; it wasn't even the transient capering of youth that he was looking for in his life's companion. After all, he was an artist, and artists wax enthusiastic about very different matters. He married her because in their marriage he found what he had been dreaming about after he'd created his inspired works of art – a wealthy father-in-law; for the the rich and refined lady's father happened to be a member of the plutocracy of Beitenzorg.

Initially, the girl's father looked at the artist with a jaundiced eye, but eventually he gave his consent to their marriage; for however much he eyed the fellow with suspicion, his daughter looked upon him from an entirely different perspective. In fact, she looked at him from *two* very different perspectives, so different, in fact, that she could never expect to land herself a better bridegroom.

Soon thereafter, the wealthy painter was discovered by the newspapers, who proceeded to make him famous.

One day, however, the artist's spouse closed her two very different eyes for ever. By then, no trace had remained of her dowry, and her father had dissociated himself completely from his son-in-law. Wolfgang was plunged into poverty of such profundity that one day, in an attempt to dodge his creditors, he swam across to Little Lagonda and became a hermit on the island.

After brief but wise meditation, he conceived of some surprisingly mundane ideas unbecoming a hermit. One such idea envisioned the establishment of a world-famous bathing resort on the tiny island. Hadn't nearby Bali been brought into vogue lately?

He decided that he must see the king about this.

The interior of the island was inhabited by a savage tribe of natives. The spectacle of the half-naked, bespectacled European sent the frightened natives running to their huts. Wolfgang went to call on King Nalaya, who was sitting in front of his tent in a puddle filled with all modern conveniences. He was a civilized native, having years before worked as stoker on board a British freighter, a fact which earned him respect among the small group of Malays he had one day come to visit, bringing the startling news that he was their king.

Only one man was found in the tribe who wanted to know the grounds for his supposed kingship, but Nalaya gave the man a trouncing sound enough to persuade the rest of the tribe to accept the inevitable.

When King Nalaya saw the blonde painter with the lobster-red face approaching, he condescendingly emitted an affable belch. Wolfgang had a shrewd idea of what he must do to assure the success of his negotiation.

"I am bringing you a present, oh Prince of the Malays," he addressed the ruler.

"Doesn't matter so long as it's nice," replied King Nalaya.

Wolfgang handed the native a block of ultramarine paint. (It was his favourite colour, and he had several more in stock.) The Malay looked at the paint.

"Nice gift," he said. "But I've already eaten one just like that. What is it you wish, oh ugly, old stranger?"

"Listen, king. Several people have written novels about neighbouring Bali Island, and those books have made the native population rich. Why shouldn't you copy their example?"

"I ain't got the knack of writing novels. And I ain't noticed nothing of the sort in my people neither."

"The novel would be written by someone else, and it would make you rich. Ever heard of something that's called advertising?"

"Ain't eaten one yet."

"It isn't something you eat. Let me tell you about advertising. People like to feel happy. I am a painter."

"I see. That's what you call advertising."

"No, it is not. Advertising is talking people into believing they'll feel pleased and happy about some things. I'll make paintings about this island, the newspapers will write about it, and entrepreneurs will fall for it. The name of the game is seaside resort. The savage tribe of white tourists, who worship a god named Baedeker, will come here visiting. That's called economic boom. Little Lagonda's going to be a seaside resort."

His Majesty became immersed in thought.

"Some brainwave, that," he said at last, using a term that was a holdover from his past as a ship's stoker.

And so they got down to work. Wolfgang swam back to Java, and got busy.

A number of ill-informed newspapermen, ignorant of the fact that the once-wealthy son-in-law had turned a half-naked hermit, accepted the new assignment, and wrote lengthy articles about the ferocious warriors of the exotic island, its lovely girls, and other local curiosities.

In due time, a loan shark had the first milk bar built on the island; the rest went like a breeze. Next came the Grand Hotel, followed by the Miami Grill, and a sprawling beach. By means of a string of million-dollar-budget films and cheap popular novels, the little South Sea island was catapulted into fame. Attractive villas were mushrooming all over the place.

The Grand Hotel was the poshest and most expensive hotel in the archipelago, a marble-and-silk marvel, with a first-rate staff, splendidly furnished rooms, bars, a restaurant, and a marina.

It so happened that one day one of the hotel's guests contracted bubonic plague. However, the guests of the Grand Hotel were people too influential and famous to be removed in order to be placed in quarantine, and so it was decided that a quarantine was to be established at the hotel itself. This is how the Grand Hotel came under quarantine.

For three whole weeks, people and animals would not be permitted to enter or leave it.

5.

Just before the quarantine was imposed, the situation in the foyer of the Grand Hotel was as follows.

Armin Vangold, a corn dealer who, having made a pile in thirty years of assiduous sales effort had decided that at last he should start living it up, and for this purpose had come to Little Lagonda with his wife Julia, was in the act of saying goodbye to his spouse at the hotel's entrance. At fifty-two, Mrs. Vangold was a straight-laced, stately 196-pound lady with an ample double chin. She was headed for the town to do some shopping, and Mr Vangold, pleading a pain in the joints, was going to stay behind. In actual fact, his joint happened to give Mr Vangold no pain on this particular day. On the contrary, finding himself in this magical palace, Mr Vangold was in the mood for enjoying, if only briefly, the easy life. He wanted to stroll about, read a magazine, have a glass of beer and – well, maybe, why not indeed? – chat up some nice lady. Surely, there was nothing wrong with that. He loved his wife, but he thought it would be nice to have a chance, once in a while, to do what he felt like doing. Oh dear, if only he could be here by himself for just a week! He would... well... drop in at the bar in the evenings. Mentioning such a thing to Julia, though, was like tempting providence.

He watched his well-built spouse retreat down the steps. She was a good wife, and he loved her very much. But, then, wasn't it true that man cannot live without water, and yet likes to have a spot of brandy now and then?

There was Lindner, the fat baritone, of whose famous voice, only one half had survived– its fame. He was just coming down the stairs from the first floor. He was asking the receptionist whether the midday mail had arrived. It had not.

Bruns, a gloomy fellow with broad shoulders and a flat nose, was standing on the stairs with his hands in his pockets, smoking a cigar. He was one of the hotel's regulars; he would come back from time to time.

Seated in one of the several large armchairs was *Signora* Relli, a Junoesque Sicilian widow with a delectable figure, whose slightly masculine voice and sharp-featured but interesting face were the perpetual focus of the hotel guests' attention. Having just lit a cigarette, she was asking the bellhop to bring her *Il Corriere della Sera*. Retired Captain Dickman of the battleship Batavia was having a chat with Hiller, a hand lotion manufacturer from Chicago. And a somewhat buxom blonde lady's luggage was just being deposited at the hotel entrance. She told the receptionist she was Mrs Hould, wife of Captain Hould, from Sydney. She was attractive, but despite all the cream and powder that had been applied to them, she had a few wrinkles at the outer corners of her eyes and on her neck. A long taut sinew would make itself visible whenever she turned her head to one side.

A well dressed young man with impeccable white skin and an interesting, handsome face was standing in one corner of the foyer. His name was Erich Kramartz. He nodded to the woman. Mrs Hould returned the greeting, then made for the lift. Just popping up was Dr Ranke, who had examined a guest who had recently become ill.

"Where can I telephone?" he enquired.

"The call-booths are on the right, sir," the receptionist offered.

The doctor hurried off. Erich Kramartz slowly started for the lift, which had just taken Mrs Hould, the newly arrived guest, to her room. The corn dealer (Mr Vangold) walked up to the reception desk, and with ostensible indifference addressed the clerk:

"Who is the blonde lady who just now entered the restaurant? She has a striking resemblance to... er... a relative of mine."

The clerk looked at him sadly.

"She is Mrs Villiers, sir. Her husband is a newspaper editor in Singapore."

Mr Vangold moved away and walked after the blonde lady with unhurried steps, like someone who was just having a look round.

Presently, a missionary came hurriedly from the restaurant. He had arrived as the member of a coach party, had just had lunch and was off, eager to get away from this glittering den of worldly sins. He wore the velvet-collared black coat of the most austere missionary order. On it, large buttons of dark stone hung loosely from their buttonholes. This garment signified that its wearer had spent years as a volunteer nurse among lepers on one of the islands.

Slowly, dreamily, the Sicilian widow ambled up to him. Taller by a head than the missionary, she flashed at him a smile displaying thirty-two perfect teeth.

"Excuse me," she said. "Am I addressing Monsignor Cresson?"

"No."

"How remarkable. You remind me of a gentleman who died recently. I thought you might be a relative. I am sorry."

She walked away.

At this moment the air was rent by a terrible wailing of sirens as a pack of some eight or ten motor vehicles came racing up to the hotel. There they screeched to a halt, and started to disgorge briskly moving soldiers and policemen.

Outside the entrance, on the street, a native Malay was hawking dance masks, gewgaws of all sorts, and postcards. Haecker, an unemployed longshoreman, was loitering outside as well, gazing at windows and things. Found among passers-by at that moment were: Miss Lidia, a lady who had been expelled by the authorities that morning after staying on the island on the plea of waiting for the return of a ship's officer who two years before had left "for just a few moments"; and Walter, the local photographer's assistant, who fancied himself a man of the world and for this reason smoked cigarettes in a holder and was carrying a riding-switch.

The soldiers jumped from the lorries and were pushing all these people into the foyer of the hotel – including Korgen, a white-bearded news vendor, who had round his neck a wire from which several illustrated magazines and newspapers were dangling, and who was getting some grating sounds out of a hurdy-gurdy he was grinding in the belief that this would boost sales of his ware.

In the foyer, these developments met with an astonished but relatively calm reception; but when an official shouted out, "Keep cool, everybody! Everything is under control!" pandemonium broke out instantly. Police took up their positions at all the hotel's exits, and a police captain loudly issued an order to a detective:

"Get all the guests down into the foyer. This hotel is under quarantine."

At this point the director showed up.

"My name is Wolfgang," he said. "It was on my order that someone called the police after the doctor had found a case of infectious disease."

"You will have to make out a report to the Chief Medical Officer. And you had better make it in writing. This outbreak, what sort of contagion is it?"

"Bubonic plague."

A number of guests had in the meantime sidled up to listen. On hearing the words "bubonic plague" they began to back away in fear of their lives.

"Only one case?" the captain asked.

"So far," the doctor commented.

Meanwhile, the Chief Medical Officer arrived. He was an obese man with a double chin that stretched from ear to ear, and was clearly suffering from asthma. The first thing he did was to enquire of the quivering receptionist (whose knees had turned to jelly) what they had to offer for lunch. He said he wanted no curry sauce with his reistaffel, for when he saw reistaffel on his plate, he could not resist the urge to tuck into it, and it disagreed with his stomach. This was an old ruse Chief Medical Officer Markheit would resort to whenever quarantine was imposed; viz.

issuing a few quick, prosaic private instructions in order to cool down the general mood of hysteria. On one occasion, in a ship that put to port under a yellow flag with eight cholera patients and a number of half-crazed passengers on board, first thing he ransacked the ship for some spirit of salt, and bitterly complained to the passengers, who were more dead than alive with terror, that he got an upset stomach, and whenever this happened he was itching all over for days on end.

"Now then, what's the matter?" Markheit enquired, turning to director Wolfgang.

"At eleven o'clock yesterday morning the doctor was called to see a guest. This morning the patient's illness was diagnosed as bubonic plague. I believe I acted in the proper way when I refrained from adopting measures to meet the emergency, as only armed force can prevent the departure of guests suspected of having contracted the disease. I ordered the two adjoining rooms locked, and left a chambermaid with the patient. That woman will have to be segregated, too, because she went upstairs to her room for a short time, not knowing as yet what it was all about. She claims she is unable to sit in hard chairs as she suffers from sciatica."

There was an infernal racket as the guests were gathering together. Many of them demanded furiously that a doctor be sent for, as they had detected symptoms of bubonic plague on themselves. The captain assured them that once the formalities had been complied with, everything would be done to make sure that they are safe and hale and hearty.

Mrs Villiers went off in a swoon, and was hanging from Captain Dickman's arm, and he was not sure what he was supposed to do with her.

The white-haired news vendor decided that the official part of the matter was over, and it was time to do business, so he started to crank his hurdy-gurdy.

This prompted a policeman to caution him in no uncertain terms that he mustn't do that.

The lift attendant was having a hysterical sobbing fit, with the result that impatient guests on upper floors were pressing buzzers in vain. The Marquis Raverdan took some medicine, and Captain Dickman deposited Mrs Villiers on the carpet behind a fancy goods seller's glass cabinet. All this while, Walter, the photographer's assistant, was issuing noisy orders, calling upon people to move farther back, and dividing them into smaller groups, like so many *tableaux vivants*.

"Ladies and Gentlemen," the captain began.

"Hear! Hear!" the photographer said encouragingly.

"The authorities have imposed quarantine at the Grand Hotel. For three weeks none of you people will be permitted to leave the premises. Any person circumventing the sanitary precautions is liable to be sentenced to a term of imprisonment of not less than five years and up to the term of his or her natural life. As a matter of fact you ought to be deported to the quarantine centre on the island of Santa Annunziata. However, the distinguished guests of this hotel have been spared that discomfort: an exception has been made, and the quarantine will be affected on these premises. For the next three weeks order will be maintained and your safety safeguarded by the joint forces of the police, the Health Service, and a detachment of the local military garrison. The authorities count upon your co-operation and understanding. We are confident that the disease will be successfully contained within this building, and that the toll will not rise."

These words triggered off a frantic rush of guests, all of whom insisted that they be given exceptional treatment. One guest claimed he stood to lose several thousand pounds sterling if he could not leave at once, and vowed to sue the government for damages. Another guest insisted that some urgent diplomatic business called him away; a third person said it was absolutely necessary for him to attend a niece's wedding party. And so on, and so forth.

"I am sorry," the captain shouted. "Not even sovereigns are permitted to violate the sanitary measures of this colony. The slightest concession in this case may sound the death knell for hundreds of thousands of people. The proprietor is obliged to provide accommodation for everyone. Persons lacking the necessary cash reserves will be staying here as guests of the government – under more modest circumstances, of course."

"I can't be compelled to stay here under more modest circumstances," said Haecker, the jobless longshoreman, whereupon the constable corrected this erroneous view in no uncertain terms.

Of all the guests, Corn dealer Vangold appeared to be the most excited.

"Look, captain," he addressed the captain distractedly. "My wife's just gone to town…"

"She won't be allowed to return here. This place has been cordoned off."

"All right, but an exceptionally energetic lady might be able to get through that cordon," Vangold said nervously.

"That's totally impossible."

The relief this statement elicited from the corn dealer was quite spectacular. Wearied and resigned to the situation, the other guests also fell silent.

At this point Wolfgang broke the silence.

"We will do our best to make the quarantine a thrilling and memorable experience to all the guests of the Grand Hotel."

6.

When Maud returned to her room, she thought the pyjama-clad stranger had left. Her relief turned to dejection as the cheeky stranger's cheerful face popped into view from behind the window curtain.

"Hello," he said by way of greeting Maud.

Once again the sound of footsteps and voices was heard outside, in the corridor.

"Why didn't you leave my room when everyone went down to the foyer?" she demanded.

"I dared not do anything without your instructions."

"Don't talk rot."

"Besides, not everyone went down to the foyer."

"What do you mean by that?"

"For instance, the person who brought you that letter," he said, pointing to the table, on which the enveloped had been placed.

Maud stood perplexed.

"Somebody was here while I was away?"

"Or so it seemed to me from my hideout under the bed."

Maud tore the envelope open and read the letter. When she had read it, she threw it into the ashtray, and touched a match to it. She watched the paper slowly burn to ashes.

"No bad news, I hope?" said the stranger in a breezy, conversational manner.

"You were an unintended witness to a conversation of which, despite all my efforts to prevent it, you must have overheard several words…"

"I assure you, it's as if…"

"Kindly hear me out… I don't know you, but I have a feeling that you are a kind-hearted person. You must have escaped from some serious trouble through my assistance. I would appreciate it if you returned my services by refraining from making enquiries about me when you've left."

"You can get that load off your mind for now," the stranger assured her. "This quarantine business is going to be on for some weeks. That'll give us plenty of time to talk things over."

"You must be kidding. Surely you don't think you're going to stay in here throughout the quarantine?"

"Where do you expect me to go?"

"How should I know? If you have no reason to be in hiding, why not take a room here?"

"I do have a reason to be in hiding! My father wants me to get married. I wanted to row a boat over to Bali island. I have a friend there who lives on the coast. He would have given me a suit of clothes."

"Where did you leave your clothes?"

"My father locked them up to prevent me getting away. My wedding was scheduled for this morning. I was going to be wearing my tails. But in the night I climbed out the window in my pyjamas, and set out for Bali. The storm drove me back to the hotel beach, and then I climbed up into this room, where I have been kept like a prisoner."

This foolish story brightened Maud up a bit, and when she spoke, it was in a friendlier manner.

"This is very sad, or funny – whichever way you choose to look at it. But you might as well reconcile yourself to your lot. The quarantine means you must give up the fight. Surely, you don't intend to hide out for weeks on end, wearing those pyjamas?"

"But what am I to tell to the hotelier when he asks me how I got in here so lightly dressed?"

"Why not tell him a lie about some amorous adventure or something?"

"All right. I'm off. Thank you for your unkind hospitality. And just for the sake of the record, you never did give me anything to eat."

For a moment they said nothing. The stranger was eyeing the letter that had turned to ashes in the ashtray.

"I wish you would trust me," he said. "I have a feeling that you're in a real fix, and the pointed-capped patent-leather shoes you chatted with aren't what you would call a man of resolution you could look to for assistance."

Maud's face registered a look of sadness.

"No," she said hesitantly. "Unfortunately, he's not in a position to help me."

"What if they arrest you?"

"What! What makes you think I'll get arrested?"

"I don't mean to bluff. I overheard you two discussing how you were to get away from here by taking a plane this evening. Now, since the quarantine constrains you to stay on, it's just possible they'll catch up with you."

"What makes you think I'm on the run from the police?"

"It's quite obvious from what I…"

Just then, there came a knock on the door.

"Who is it?"

"The police."

7.

Quickly and noiselessly, the pyjama-clad stranger slipped under the bed.

"Come in," Maud called out cheerfully.

"Gosh," the pyjamas thought in amazement. "There's a woman for you! Such sang-froid! Absolutely one of a kind."

A pair of round-capped manufactured shoes appeared in his field of vision between two legs of the bed.

"I am sorry to break in on you like this. I am Chief Inspector Elder."

"Maud Borckman. Won't you sit down." The pair of buckled walking shoes moved.

"Thank you," said Round-Capped Shoes. "Well, Miss Borckman, the questioning of the guests is going on in the foyer, actually. But to speed up the procedure, I have taken on some of the more important questioning."

"Why is it necessary to question people in a quarantine?"

One of the buckled walking shoes disappeared. Apparently Maud had crossed her legs.

"Ah!" replied Round-Capped Shoes hoarsely. "This has nothing to do with the quarantine! Miss Borckman, weren't you aware that while the guests were hurrying downstairs to the foyer, someone was murdered next door to you, in Number 71?"

The other walking shoe reappeared. She must have put her foot down in surprise.

"What! Who?"

"Dr Ranke."

"But how could he...? This is so strange... I am sorry that *I* am asking *you* a question."

"I can understand you, Miss Borckman. Somebody stabbed Dr Ranke to death. Room Number 70 is unoccupied. Your room, Number 72, is the other adjoining room. There are no other rooms in this part of the corridor... I say, there's a smell of burnt paper here."

"I received a letter in which an annoying communication was made. I burnt it."

"Such sang-froid," thought Pyjamas. "Such perfect self-control!"

"Is there a pneumatic post in this hotel?" the chief inspector asked.

"I don't know. The letter came by ordinary mail."

"That's odd. The quarantine headed off today's mail."

There was a long pause.

"I don't understand it," Maud said pleasantly. "It lay here, on the table. Perhaps it came in yesterday's mail."

"Perhaps it did. May I ask your a few formalities? Your name?"

"Maud Borckman."

"Born?"

"1919"

"Where?"

There was a pause.

"In Achinsk – er – Russia."

"That's a place in Siberia, isn't it?"

"Yes."

"Domiciled... Your place of residence?"

"In Surabaya. I work for the National Institute of Chemistry. I am an assistant to Professor Decker."

"Indeed? Oh, I am a great admirer of the professor. He is a genius. Are you on holiday here?"

Another pause ensued.

"No. I've quit my job."

As he was lying on his stomach under the bed, Felix Van der

Gullen, the impertinent stranger, was aware of a very bitter taste in his mouth. There was something wrong here, he thought. There was something very, very wrong about this wonderful, attractive young woman. She was lying, do doubt about that. There was trouble in the air.

By contrast, Round-Capped Shoes with the hoarse voice appeared to be far less suspicious. He virtually ignored Walking Shoes' embarrassment.

"Ah well," he said reassuringly. "These are just routine questions. If you find them embarrassing, you don't have to answer them. As far as we are concerned, there is only one question that is of importance. We know that the murder was committed while the quarantine order was being read to the guests. Prior to that, the doctor was seen, and about fifteen minutes later, he was dead. Consequently, all that we need to do is to find out where the occupants in this hotel were during those critical fifteen minutes."

Silence reigned. One walking shoe disappeared. So Maud had regained her self-control.

"I see," she said in her pleasant, clear voice that managed to convey indifference and almost sounded breezy.

"It's a quite simple procedure. Now will you please tell me where you were staying while the quarantine was being announced?"

"I was here, in this room."

Under the bed, the man in the pyjamas became petrified. Hey, what was this? he asked himself.

"So that's settled. Of course, the detective knocked on the door, asking you to come down to the foyer?"

"Yes, he did."

"Did you have any reason to stay on in here all the same?"

"Nothing particular. From the window I saw the soldiers arrive with wire fencing. I lived in India for fifteen years, so I knew what was up and – well, I just don't like being in attendance at official procedures."

"Ah. I see. Now it's perfectly clear." The chief inspector appeared to be in full agreement with her attitude. "Guests staying at a fashionable hotel care little about formalities."

"Unfortunately, one little suspects beforehand that one's presence may be of importance subsequently."

"Naturally, naturally," agreed the chief inspector like a

solicitous hairdresser's assistant. "But fortunately, I've had extensive experience in such matters, and I am well aware that an unexpected quarantine may frequently produce surprises of a tragic nature. Many's the time that criminals and hotel thieves have taken advantage of the panicky atmosphere of the first few moments. For this reason, I always hasten to draw up a list of all the persons who were present when the quarantine was announced."

"Oh, do you? How very ingenious."

"Thank you. Let me ask just one more question. It's just a formality, but it'll make our job easier. Did you by any chance have a visitor here when the detective knocked on your door? An alibi is always so much more simple for us to accept if there is a witness."

There was a pause, however brief, and the sound of a lighter being lit.

"No. I had no visitor."

"Ah. I'm glad that I know that. These employees here are so foolish. One lift attendant says he saw Prince Sergius in the corridor, and that he seemed to have come from your room. A lot of trash, of course. These attendants are talking a lot of drivel. Telling cock and bull stories because they want to look important."

"The prince did come to see me in this room. It was some ten minutes before the quarantine. But when the attendant knocked, he had gone. He said he was going to call on Mr Vangold, the corn dealer. They are acquainted. Possibly, Mr Vangold had gone downstairs by then. The prince must have emerged from *his* room. Third room as the corridor turns. Number 70. That's Mr Vangold's room."

"Yes, I know. In fact the attendant did say that that room might be the one from which the prince had emerged, but I didn't think so. However, since he didn't come from your room, I must accept that he had come from Mr Vangold's."

"Number 70 is the only room he could have come from."

"That's interesting, because, as a matter of fact, the murder was committed there."

8.

A long, benumbed silence followed these words. The gentleman under the bed felt as if someone had grabbed him by the throat.

"But you said Dr Ranke was murdered in Number 71," he heard the girl say.

"Now did I indeed? It was a mistake. It happened in Number 70, Mr Vangold's room. Your room is Number 72, and Number 71 is unoccupied."

That was a nasty trap, and no mistake. The painful atmosphere in the room was now quite palpable.

A chair creaked.

"Well," Round-Capped Shoes said affably. "I think we've done with the formalities. It's good to get such things over and done with. I am sorry to have disturbed you."

"It's all right." There was a creaking again. "By the way," Maud said, "I did not actually *see* the prince after he had left this room. I only *assumed* that he had come from Mr Vangold's room."

"Of course. I'm not going to put that on record. The name of such a respectable, distinguished person must not be brought into the remotest connection with this affair."

"That's what I think, too."

"I'm glad we are of one mind. I am a great admirer of the prince. Lord Shilling, the governor of Tonga Island, for whom I've had the opportunity to render some services, promised me this morning to introduce me to the prince at lunch. But this unfortunate business of the quarantine had deprived me of the honour."

"You mean to say you didn't come here as a member of the quarantine party?"

"By no means. I had been investigating a different case and, like yourself, I'm trapped here by the quarantine."

"Is there... Was another criminal act committed in this hotel?"

"Not in this hotel. The footprints of the most vicious criminal in the archipelago led to this hotel. In the underworld they call him the 'Terror of Java'. He is a violent type, one who robs and kills with utmost cruelty. And he is a deceptively pleasant-looking man. He was last seen in the hotel garden. If only I could be sure that he's around here somewhere, I wouldn't have to worry about the identity of the murderer. Oddly enough, I found this white horn button lying by the side of Dr Ranke's body. It looks like one of those buttons one finds on night garments. Don't you think so?"

"White horn buttons aren't sewn on men's clothing."

"Not on morning wear, no. But one would expect to find buttons like this on pyjamas, and the guilty party was wearing pyjamas when he gave me the slip. However, it is possible that he fled in some other direction. It would be too lucky a coincidence if he fell into my hands owing to this quarantine."

The round-capped shoes now touched at the ankles, indicating that their wearer was making a bow.

The sound of the door being opened could be heard.

"Pleased to have met you," Maud said.

"Should you have anything you'd wish to tell me, Miss Borckman, you can trust me. I'm not a heartless sleuth."

The door was closed. When Maud turned, she found the pyjama-clad stranger seated in the armchair, smoking a cigarette.

9.

She eyed him silently.

"What is it?" said the young man. Receiving no reply, he went on. "Well," he said, and his words carried appreciation, "I sure have caught it from him. Now, what do you think of me as the 'Terror of Java'?"

"Did you kill Dr Ranke?"

Maude had spoken softly, without a hint of reproach.

"Before I answer that, may I ask *you* a question?"

"Go ahead."

"Did *you* kill Dr Ranke?"

"Listen. I must warn you that there is a limit to my patience. Too much is at stake now for me to protect you in order to avoid unpleasant appearances."

"You're right. From now on you will protect me on a quid pro quo basis. You see, I *know* you were *not* alone in this room when the detective knocked on the door to notify you that quarantine had been imposed. I know that you were *not* in this room when the murder was committed, and I also know that Prince Sergius had *not* left this room when the detective came. Where were you during those fifteen minutes after you had left the room?

Because, you see, you weren't in the foyer and neither were you in this room. The same goes for the prince."

"I was on my way to the foyer, but turned back."

"You did, did you? Then why didn't you tell that to the detective?"

At this Maud lost her patience.

"How dare you ask *me* questions? A man a chief inspector of the police refers to as the worst scoundrel on this continent! One who got away in his night clothes to escape the gallows!"

"I would have preferred to escape by plane to Singapore."

That remark hit home. Maud turned white, and said nothing. The stranger got up.

"Look here," he said gently. "Why don't we make peace? Or if you like, let's contract an alliance."

"With you? Now listen. My unfortunate circumstances may prevent me from turning you over to the police, but I will not make common cause with scoundrels. If you think I am one of your kind, you're quite mistaken."

"All right. Then why not make an agreement? We will both keep what we know about the other under wraps. Is that a deal?"

Maud lowered her voice to a whisper.

"Did *you* kill him?" she asked, horrified. "Please, reply. I... I won't... give you away."

The stranger reflected for a while. She stepped closer to him, and fixed a glassy look at his pyjama jacket.

He automatically followed her stare.

One white horn button was missing.

10.

"So it was you... Please... For heaven's sake... If you ever were a God-fearing man, tell them it was you. I beseech you."

He eyed her, then slowly nodded.

"All right."

Maud heaved a sigh of relief.

"But why?"

"He recognized me. Once in Batavia, I broke into a house where Dr Ranke happened to be a guest. I was arrested. He saw me again at my trial, so he had ample opportunity to memorize my face. As I walked out of this room, he was coming towards me from the far end of the corridor. I always carry a dagger on me… I made a stab, and that was the end of him."

She contemplated him in horror. This nice-looking, affable man was a heinous murderer! He had talked about his foul deed as if it had been a prank. She wondered why it hurt her so much. She ought to be glad to know that it wasn't Sergius who had done it.

"You murdered him! You killed a man in cold blood!"

He shrugged nonchalantly.

"One more fellow done in makes no difference."

"Go away! Please go. Leave here at once!"

Daylight was beginning to fade. The garden was choked up with guests. They had grown accustomed to the quarantine, and were passing jokes with the soldiers encamped on the other side of the barbed wire fence. Only a little posse of hypochondriacs, headed by Mrs Villiers (whose husband was a newspaper editor in Singapore) were falling from one faint into another in their rooms, or checking their bodies for symptoms of and official tones that some of the guests had their minutes numbered.

It was the end of the season, and at dusk the heavy, misty air already came surging from the direction of the sea, and overlay the palm leaves and the extended chalices of colourful hibiscuses and orchids with a greasy sheen. Rolling, evil-smelling hot air currents, forerunners of the north-western monsoon. brought the stench of tree-roots rotting along the seashore.

At this time of year the smell of the tropical paradise being transformed into hell on earth could still only be smelt in the languor-inducing, muggy dusk air, as it blew inland in breaths of the invading monsoon that came with the incoming tide. A few more days – or perhaps in just a few more hours, for in these parts the season changes abruptly – and the weather would be apoplexy-inducing like this day in and day out.

The reflection of the departing sun as it was sinking into the sea filled with shadows the room in which two trapped persons were standing silently, facing each other.

"This is the right moment, I think," said the man in pyjamas. He took a soap and a towel from off the edge of the washbasin in the room. "Will you just peek out to see if the coast is clear."

Maud opened the door a crack.

"Now!" she whispered quickly.

"I'm sorry I have intruded upon you," he said, and stepped

out of the room. He started down the corridor, walking with the self-assurance of a hotel guest.

Maud leaned with her back against the closed door, and shut her eyes.

"Oh my God," was her first thought.

Then she reached into the décolletage of her dress and brought out from it a small lace cover, such as is found on the small table in each room. She unfolded it – and there dropped from it a small, blood-stained dagger with a metal handle.

11.

Towel over one arm and a soap-holder in the other, Felix hurried down the corridor. The personnel, in view of the approaching off-season, had been halved, and the reduced staff proved to be alarmingly insufficient since, along with the official functionaries, there were numerous non-resident guests in the restaurant, the bar, and the foyer, who had to be accommodated. During the high season bellhops and chambermaids were plentiful at the Grand Hotel. But when the most punctual of guests – the monsoon – arrives, it finds the staff diminished, and influential people and celebrities stay away.

Misfortunes do not come singly; an added misfortune for the hotel was a group of tourists who had arrived by motor-coach just for lunch, and would have returned to Surabaya in the evening. Among them were the Reverend Paulo Sorgette, a hulking, white-haired Jesuit missionary, the Baronet Culson, and Mr Jenkins, the sugar baron and regatta champion.

Director Wolfgang could look forward to a whopping big extra income, for the guests of the Grand Hotel could be trusted not to avail themselves of the food and the cheap little rooms that would be paid for by the government; they would continue to live in grand style, spending lavishly. What a fabulous income!

By contrast, Felix, the 'Terror of Java', wearing pyjamas and with soap-dish in hand, was heading, apparently full of assurance, for some place he hadn't the faintest idea of, very much pleased about corridors and passages that, because of a lack of personnel, appeared deserted. There was little danger, as newly arrived residents were plentiful, so who would be suspicious of a man in pyjamas who was hurrying down corridors, carrying a soap-dish?

A black-skinned boy in a gilded cap was coming towards him. He turned out to be the lift attendant. He might remember the man he had brought up to the floor.

Felix stopped.

"Eh, lad. Can you tell me the time, please?" he shouted at the boy, and by way of bantering lightly flapped his face with the towel.

"It's two minutes past six o'clock, *mynheer*."

"Thank you." Felix strode on, humming a tune. He quickly walked in through a door above which a sign said "Bathroom".

Damn it, Felix thought. Something would have to be done at last! For one thing, he was starving to death; for another, if he was going to have to keep on this cock-sure rushing about with the towel for much longer, he was sure to die the death of an exhausted marathon runner.

He heard the humming noise of a descending lift.

Ah, so that infernal brat was at last on his way down to the blasted ground floor! He emerged from the bathroom, and cautiously looked around. First of all, he had to lay hold of some clothing. But how on earth was he to lay his hands on it? Right before him, a door was opening, sending him moving briskly on, flapping his towel.

He turned the corner and went up the stairs to the next floor. There he stopped, panting.

And now who should be coming towards him but that blasted lift attendant? That damned lift had just happened to halt at this floor. Amazement was written all over the blighter's face.

It was back to the trot for Felix. This sort of thing wouldn't do. Trembling at the knees, he trotted around the corridor and came to another bathroom. In you go!

Bang! That shelter was locked. What was to be done now?

Again, a door opened just opposite, and he was on the point of starting off again on his purposeful hurrying when he saw a hand reach out to put out a pair of large shoes. That done, the door closed.

From a clothes-peg above the shoes, a few pieces of clothing were hanging in a disorderly bundle.

It was a hit-or-miss business. This man would sleep until next morning; surely, he wouldn't need these clothes until then. He was going to borrow them, put them on, and then he would be able to go down to the foyer, and have some food. He would eat. EAT!

Afterwards he would bring the clothes back. Room Number 166 – that was all he needed to remember. He must go ahead and grab them. There was no other way!

He snatched the clothes from the peg, and was off. Behind him he heard the lift humming. Look alive, old man, he told himself. This pestilential attendant chap was coming up again!

As he was turning a dark corner, he glimpsed an iron stairway. The winding stairs started from a narrow opening in the wall. Hanging from the ceiling was a sign which said:

> **SERVICE STAIRS.
> NOT FOR USE
> BY GUESTS**

This was tailor-made for him. He was no guest.

He ran up several stairs, and with the bundle of clothes in his lap, sat down to catch his breath.

"Hey, Marti-i-i-n!" The highly unpleasant, screeching female voice came from way down below.

"What is it?" a vexed Felix shouted back.

"That you?"

"Aha..."

The female down below seemed reassured. She was making clattering noises with some things. She must be either on the ground floor or in the cellar.

Who on earth was that Martin fellow he was being mistaken for?

Now for those clothes! Put them on, man, look alive!

He was famished. He quickly kicked off one of his slippers.

"Marti-i-i-in!"

She would never stop this.

"What is it again?"

"You still there?"

"I'm not. But may be back any minute," he replied angrily.

"You're always horsing around."

God, was she spinning it out! He made no reply. He quickly took off the other slipper, and started to put on the clothes.

33

"Hey, Marti-i-i-in!"

Confound that Martin fellow!

"What do you want?"

"When you come down, don't forget to bring the master key. I can't go fetch it. I left it in me room."

Good heavens! Was she yelling, that damned woman!

"All right. I'll bring it. Anything else?"

"You could bring smoked fish. Throw the lot down, into the wash room. But you be careful. When they bring the bed sheet upstairs, you put new washing on the stair."

He had the trousers on. They were a bit loose-fitting, the kind of thing old-fashioned gentlemen would wear. The coat flapped round his knees. A frock coat, for goodness sake! Something of a rarity in the tropics.

He folded his pyjamas and placed them on the top stair. No one could be expected to come up this way.

"Marti-i-i-in! Marti-i-i-in!"

She would awaken the whole hotel, that hussy.

"What do you want?"

"You be careful! No one must see you throw things into the washroom!"

"All right. I'll be careful."

"I'm expecting you tomorrow again, Marti-i-i-in."

"My pleasure."

Drat that blighter Martin and his woman! He felt dizzy from hunger. Slowly, he went down the four steps to reach the corridor.

"Marti-i-i-in!"

He wished she would choke. He congealed into a piece of statuary, and made no reply.

"You don't hear, Marti-i-i-in? Ah and drop me…"

Wouldn't I drop you from a height, he thought wishfully.

"… drop me a coral pearl, Marti-i-i-in. You find it hanging beside the mirror. Mind you don't push over the vase."

Silence fell. He heard a door slammed shut downstairs. That fiendish slut was gone.

Cautiously, he peered out – then quickly pulled his head back. That black-skinned brat was standing by the lift, chewing on a straw and spitting it out bit by tiny bit.

As a matter of fact, he could as well descend by the winding staircase. The woman who had been shouting up to him had been quite far below, and she wasn't there anymore.

Very slowly, he started down the iron stairs. On reaching the second floor he looked down. Down below, in the darkness of the bottom, farther down than the ground floor corridor, he saw a bright round spot of light on the ground. That must be where the voice had come from.

A way should be found to change his face. How easily such a feat is done in novels, and how utterly impossible it is in real life!

At the first floor, he heard several voices, and halted. As they were coming nearer, he heard a rattling noise. Was it a sword?... Aha, it was the captain.

"The result of the interrogations is negative. They have alibis, all of them. And those who were in their room are above suspicion."

Chief Inspector Elder was standing behind the police officers.

"If you ask me, every person is suspect so long as he or she cannot produce an alibi," he interposed.

The captain turned to face him.

"I'd rather you didn't concern yourself with this matter, Elder," he said somewhat icily. "Here, in the Grand Hotel, one has to adopt a special manner of procedure. An indiscretion, a blunder or a scandal could entail consequences that I'd rather not think about."

"Oh no. Good heavens. On no account would I interfere with your business, captain. It would be superfluous anyway, since it is your team that is carrying on the investigation. On the contrary, I believe *I* shall need help from *you* people."

They eyed him with suspicion. Though he was a young man, Chief Inspector Elder had gained considerable popularity in the colony as something of a romantic hero. According to the captain, Elder owed his reputation to sheer good luck and to his affected manners. High-ranking police officers had been by-passed when delicate political affairs or major criminal cases were assigned to the chief inspector instead, and his colleagues had never forgiven him.

"If we can be of any help to you, just tell us," the captain replied. "Even though I am not acquainted with the nature of your assignment."

"If my investigation should come to a dead end, and unfortunately it looks like it will, I'll ask you people to help me. This time I seem to be out of luck."

"Was questioning Miss Borckman part of your assignment?" one of the officers asked.

"Let me warn you, Elder. If, contrary to regulations, you should attempt to interfere with the matter that's been assigned to my group…"

"I assure you, it was in execution of my assignment that I saw Miss Borckman. I am looking for a man who was prowling about in the garden here, and who may have climbed through a window into one of the rooms. For this reason, I have questioned several resident guests, and now I am no longer interested in anything. I'm going to turn in. Good night."

"There goes the great charlatan of crime fighting," remarked one of the officers when Elder had gone. "He's like a quack doctor. A master of make-believe. But what did you expect? Serious work is never appreciated as much as quackery and eyewash are."

"Well, gentlemen," said the captain. "Lieutenant Sedlintz will be on duty. If possible, keep the investigation low-key. Tomorrow, we shall have to find out who may have had an interest in Dr Ranke being murdered."

"And we'll have to look for the dagger," one officer interposed. "The murderer took it away with him. Find the dagger and you'll have the murderer."

"You're right. Check the sentries, Sedlintz, but proceed with tact. Be careful. This is the Grand Hotel. Good night."

Clattering. The sound of doors being shut. The police officers had gone to bed.

The 'Terror of Java,' the cheeky stranger, resumed his descent on the winding stairs. This staircase was unlit. Apparently, it wasn't used in the evening. What a shame, skimping on lighting this way! That fellow Martin and his lady were risking their lives whenever they were having one of these trysts of theirs here.

He must have reached the ground floor. The basement was under his feet. He heard some voices and rattling noises down below. What was down there? The servants' quarters?

"Don't you dare attempt it," whispered a voice.

"There's nothing I can do. I'm afraid. Police all over the place."

"You needn't be afraid. The police have gone to bed. They won't ever come here. Now speak up, or else!"

"I don't know nothing. I just seen Miss Borckman, she take the knife. Wrapped it in a small white lace cover."

"Then *she* is the murderer!"

Felix stood benumbed. He felt as if the hotel were crawling with ghosts. Should he go down to the basement? If he made just one move, he'd frighten these people away. They had gone down to the basement to discuss things. He withdrew to the backstairs. They were whispering heated words, and he could hear everything quite clearly.

"You'd better tell that to the detectives tomorrow."

"No, no. They find out everything, and then they send us all to jail."

"Ma-a-rti-i-i-in."

Damn it! He'd frightened them away.

The pair of whisperers separated and leaped backwards. Receding footsteps could be heard. Felix dared not move.

"Ma-ar-ti-i-i-in. Why you don't drop fish, coral, key?... You hear, Martin?" Silence. She was walking away, muttering angrily: "You no hear, Marti-i-i-in. You just eat and sleep. Damn fool. Dirty pig. Just you wait."

There was a truly refined lady for you, the young man was thinking. This chap Martin should be more discriminating in his choice of women.

He stepped out into the ground-floor corridor. In any case, there *was* something wrong with that pretty young lady. If she did have the dagger on her, and they were going to report her to the police, then she was finished. Something ought to be done about this.

First of all, he was going to have something in the way of nourishment... Now why was this place so dark?

He bumped into something. It was a table. Light was filtering in on the side, and he could make out several more tables. This boded no good. It was the hotel dining hall, and apparently dinner was over. The sound of jazz music came very softly from somewhere.

It was the Bar and Grill of the Grand Hotel. This spot was not likely to be crowded with people tonight. Never mind. What mattered was that they offered first-class cuisine.

He quietly emerged into the foyer. Lighting was down to economy level. It was a spacious, deserted hall. Far down, the receptionist was leaning against a shelf, reading something. Felix remembered that he was wearing no neck-tie. The collar of a nightshirt would do in the tropics, but only if you had a tie on. He spotted a punkah on one of the tables, a type of electric fan

37

with long silk ribbons tied to it. The ribbons were fluttering horizontally when the fan was in operation. He tore off one ribbon, and quickly made it into a bow tie. It was a bit old-fashioned, the sort of thing artists would wear in days of old, but then everyone dressed as they damn well pleased.

He calmly started for the bar. The receptionist looked up, but seeing that the guest wasn't coming in his direction, resumed his reading.

The hunted game named Felix entered the so-called grill, which opened from the foyer.

He came into a room dimly lit by blue lights. It was filled with the sound of excellent tango music – and chock-full of people. Gowns rustled and shoes shuffled, scraping on the glass floor lit from underneath, and in the air the fragrance of flavoured cigarette smoke blended with the faint smell of food. An accordion was emitting whining strains. The clinking of glasses and the clatter of plates at times would drown out the sound of soft conversations. The spotlight changed to red... There was a burst of laughter, quick, staccato – it was the Sicilian widow's irrepressible joie de vivre triggered by a precipitate movement of Mr Vangold's that landed the pincer of a crab in the lap of Governor Shilling. In the semi-darkness high-spirited gentlemen were sitting at tables, magnificent jewels were glittering, and flashing like glow-worms, wonderful Parisian dresses conjured into garments from small handfuls of fabrics were rustling under the green-and-violet lights that were projected onto the dance-floor. Female shoulders, smooth backs and uncovered arms, some of them dark-complexioned, others lily-white, stood out from the darkness in high relief.

Felix walked up to the bar. The Tamil mixer grinned at him.

"A glass of champagne on the rocks. Plenty of rocks," commanded the hungry, cheeky – and haunted – stranger.

A moment later the glass was placed in front of him, ice cubes slid into it clattering from a bone jug. The manageress, a gorgeous Belgian blonde, stepped up to him. Because of the dimmed tango lighting that was directed on the dance-floor, everything was wrapped in shadow, but even so Felix was able to see that he was facing a very slender woman.

"My name is Odette Dufleur. When you come to the Grill, you are my guest."

"In that case we shall see a lot of each other."

He put down his glass, though he was dying to have a spot of ice-cool champagne.

"Do you dance?" Odette Dufleur inquired.

"Certainly. May I have the pleasure?"

They were tangoing in the deep violet-coloured light of the dance floor.

"You are a very good dancer," the manageress whispered.

"I love music. But the principal reason is that I happen to have a light and exquisite partner who is a truly marvellous dancer... What's this scent you're wearing on your hair? Lantheric? No. It's Chalimar."

"Right. You *are* a great connoisseur of perfumes."

For a second darkness and silence fell on the premises, then the intimacy of the place was shattered as the bar exploded into blinding light. With a light habitual gesture, the hunted game threaded Mlle Odette's hand through his arm, and walked up to his glass of champagne. He laid hold of the slender glass.

How odd that people here don't applaud when a piece has been performed, he thought. What was stranger still, they seemed to have become mute. Holding his glass, he looked around.

What had happened?

Men and women froze in mid-motion as they riveted their eyes on him. Mlle Odette, her small red lips parted, stared at Felix in alarm.

The young man stood benumbed, holding his glass. He was aware that something disastrous must have happened.

At last he glimpsed his image in the mirror opposite, and the spectacle sent shivers down his spine.

He was standing at the bar counter, holding a glass of champagne – and was wearing the velvet-collared black garb of the strictest missionary order.

12.

Yes, there he was standing before an assemblage of dumbfounded people dressed in that velvet-hemmed black garb with square stone buttons on it, a person who might have done a stint of at least five years amongst lepers, a person who had turned his back on all worldly pleasures, which he abhorred... And he was clutching a champagne glass, having just finished dancing a tango!

The bombshell was about to explode. It would be a scandal of unprecedented scale, followed by an arrest... The thought made him shudder.

Suddenly, he lifted his glass high, and started to speak in a stentorian voice.

"Listen ye revellers!" he sang out. "The portent of death has this day appeared in this house! I came here so that I might be the invisible hand on the wall of Belshazzar's palace. Remember that the plague causes the handwriting appear on the wall amid marble columns, silk curtains and gilded tapestries just as it does on the walls of the humblest fisherman's hut: '*Mene, mene, tekel, upharsin.*' I have come to dance in your midst, to make merry amongst you, in the hope that in this way perhaps your deaf ears will hear, and your unseeing eyes will see Death, and so ...."

Amid the horrified silence, he raised his champagne glass, and dashed it to the floor. He let his eyes rove around the frightened assemblage of people, and as he was leaving, added:

"That was the reason why I ordered the champagne. I ordered it so that I might destroy it, champagne being a symbol of worldly sin."

The mixer, awe-struck and terrified, whispered:

"I understand that. But what did you want rocks in it for?"

The grim missionary made no reply as, with firm steps, he strode from the bar.

13.

Prince Sergius, who was sitting with Maud in one of the boxes, reflected.

"These fanatics," he said to her. "Last year, in Singapore, a missionary ran onto the stage in a music-hall and began to dance in the chorus line. It was a dreadful sight."

Maud said nothing

Little by little the depression that the unexpected disturbance had caused in the bar was easing off.

"Such behaviour is against regulations," said Councillor Markheit, who was dining in Mrs Villiers's company, after ascertaining that she had not contracted bubonic plague. "If he weren't a missionary, his conduct would amount to a misdemeanour. Creating panic in a quarantined place is a serious offence."

"Who is this person?" the Sicilian widow enquired excitedly

of Mr Vangold, whose acquaintance she had made by chance. The corn dealer was thoroughly upset by his wife's absence, so much so that in his black mood he was absent-minded enough to sit down to *Signora* Relli's table to have dinner. The markedly beautiful widow had permitted him to stay on with her even after the misunderstanding had been clarified.

After dinner, they chanced to drop in at the bar to "just sit around for some time".

"He's a missionary," replied Vangold. "That's all I know."

"Peter!" the *Signora* called to the waiter.

"*Signora?*"

"Who is this missionary?"

"I have no idea, ma'am. So many people arrived today," the waiter said, and hurried off, as guests were asking for their bills at several tables. Director Wolfgang was thinking all sorts of things about the missionary.

"You seem to be keenly interested in missionaries."

"Indeed I am. When I was a girl, I fell in love with a missionary. Alas, there was little chance of my parents letting me marry him, and so he left and took up a post among the savages. My late husband was a good man, and intelligent, and he loved me, but I've never been able to forget Cresson. Ever since I became a widow, I've been a frequent visitor in these parts, as missionaries are plentiful here, and so many of them – er – resemble him."

"You hope to be able to see him again?" Mr Vangold asked.

"He died. He became a victim of his vocation, and I've sunk a portion of my fortune in the sepulchral monument I ordered erected in his native town."

"Did you have his mortal remains brought home?" asked Mr Vangold, touched.

"I didn't," replied the widow icily. Then after a brief pause she added: "He was eaten by the savages."

Lindner, the opera singer, who was just passing, stopped by their table.

"I don't like missionaries of this sort," he said, and his chubby face assumed a sad, childish expression. "Now I'll have to take a sleeping-pill again. And I'd been feeling quite all right."

"Better take no sleeping-pills," said the widow with authority. "Come and join us... Peter, bring us a bottle of Cinzano!... This is Signor Lindner... Mr Vangold."

"Pleased to meet you," said the corn merchant, and rose to shake hands with the singer. "When I was a young man, I used to be a great admirer of your voice. You sang *Lohengrin* marvellously. And what a good-looking guy you were. Oh dear, the good old days!"

He sighed. He was puzzled to see the great artiste turn decidedly frosty as he sat down to the table.

"We will now drain our glasses," *Signora* Relli prompted the men, raising her glass filled with ruby-red vermouth. They drank up. Lindner did so, too, although he didn't much fancy it. *Signora* Relli stood up.

"You will excuse me, gentlemen," she said, and hurriedly left the bar.

"She is a nice person," Vangold remarked, and refilled their glasses. He was having a killingly good time. The drinks were something he wasn't used to and, well… This *Signora* Relli made really excellent company. "You had a prodigious voice in days of old," he said, addressing Lindner, anxious to please the celebrated artiste. "What a pity you've lost it. Do you think it's gone for good? I knew a teacher… he also acted as parish choir-master. He lost his voice, too, but after a time it cleared again. The same thing may happen to you!"

"Impossible," Lindner replied, and his face was ghastly pale. "Nervousness harms one's voice, and I am irritated to death by drivelling prattlers."

"Oh, really? Now that's the way *I* feel about my store man. Whenever I tell him, 'I say. Mr Stuck, will you please bring up…'"

"What's keeping *Signora* Relli?" said the singer impatiently.

"I believe she's looking for that missionary fellow, the one who just gave us all such a good dressing-down."

Mr Vangold guessed right. *Signora* Relli, as she emerged into the foyer, took a look round. She spotted the missionary seated at a small table, deep in conversation with the waiter.

"I am going to have dinner here. I refuse to set foot in that den of iniquity," Felix said, casting a longing glance in the direction of the bar.

"We are pleased to serve food out here," the waiter said. "But all we've got left in the kitchen is half a slice of thin fish, which the cook had laid aside for herself. She's on a slimming cure."

"You mean, there's no fish stocked in a smart hotel like this?"

"Alas, we didn't expect missionary guests. Our guests are sinners, all of them, and though it's Friday, they refuse to have meatless dishes, even today. For this reason we have on our bill of fare nothing but dishes Monsignor would reject in disgust – things like roast beef, chicken cutlet with curry sauce, or turkey. Dishes of that sort."

The very thought of a bit of roast beef – to say nothing of cutlet (with curry sauce) – positively made the missionary's mouth water.

"Bring me that bit of fish, cooked in water," he commented sadly.

He sat at the small table, wearing a mournful expression and trying to fight off an urge to tear his hair out.

"Sorry to disturb you, Reverend Father. My name is Mrs Relli, widowed," said a voice at close quarters.

He looked up and saw before him a stately, Junoesque woman with marked features but a pretty face, with dangerously flashing eyes and large, white teeth.

"I am still under the influence of your sermon. What you did just now was so terrifying and yet so magnificent..."

"Fighting the worldly sins," he said, impatiently looking about to see if the waiter was bringing his food. He felt a keen yearning even for that meatless dish, and wished the waiter hurry it up.

"I need someone... a person I can talk to in all sincerity. If you think you can spare me half an hour, I beg you to listen to what I have to say to you."

"I am now going to have dinner," he announced, having perceived that the waiter was bringing him his fish.

"I must! I must talk to a rigorous missionary with flaming eyes, one to whom I can open my heart wide any lay bare the secrets that are hidden in my soul..."

Unfortunately, it was her bare arms that she opened wide, and as she did not look behind her, she knocked the platter from the waiter's hands. The little bit of cooked fish rested motionless in a puddle of soup on the carpet.

"O Santa Madonna!" she exclaimed in despair. "How clumsy of me! Please, permit me to invite you to a cup of tea as a small compensation for your dinner. Please don't turn me down, Father.

You would humiliate me if you did. My room is Number 20. It's quite nearby."

"Please... er... I must not eat anything but a meatless dish today," he said, broken-hearted, viewing the fish on the floor with a look of profound grief as one looks at a beloved relative who has just departed this life.

With a curt nod to *Signora* Relli and an empty stomach below his stern mien, he turned and started for the main staircase.

Then, making a sudden turn-about, he entered the darkened restaurant.

14.

For a fleeting moment, Elder caught sight of the fugitive cleric. Quickly, he walked up to the receptionist.

"Do you know that missionary?"

"I suppose so, sir. But there have been too many arrivals today, so I'll have to look him up in the book if you wish to know something about him."

"I do. I want to know his name and other particulars."

Meanwhile, the head waiter had come out from the bar and went up to *Signora* Relli.

"Will you please come back to the bar, ma'am. The two gentlemen at your table are loudly calling each other names."

"O Santa Madonna!" she exclaimed, and hurried back to the bar, with the head waiter trailing close behind her.

"The Reverend Paul Sorgette, Missionary," announced the receptionist. "He arrived by motor-coach with a party of excursionists from Java and entered the Grand Hotel for a banking transfer. This regrettable incident has kept him here."

"What is his room number?"

"Number 66. Second floor."

Elder walked up to the restaurant door, but found that it was locked. Without hesitation he went to the lift and entered the car.

"Second floor," he commanded, and the lift started to move with a humming noise.

He could have kicked himself for not having followed the missionary right away.

The lift stopped, and he made to get out.

"You can't, sir," said the black-skinned boy attendant. "We're stuck between floors."

"Why did the lift stop?"

"Probably somebody opened the door on one of the floors."

"What d'you do now?" Elder stamped his feet impatiently.

"We'll press the buzzer for the receptionist. He'll walk up to each floor and shut the open door. Then we'll be on our way again. He moves awfully slow, that guy. If the lift door actually opened on one of the top floors, we'll stay in here till the small hours. Fact is, he's got sciatica, poor fish. It's tough on a receptionist. I'm sure I would fire him if I was the boss."

"Did you press the bell button?"

"Not yet. But it's something I do in no time," the attendant said reassuringly, and pressed one of several white buttons. "Now just watch what a long time the old geezer's going to take, pottering about."

Indeed it took the receptionist half an hour to climb up to all five floors before realizing that he had forgotten to check the mezzanine. It was there that the door had gotten opened.

The lift shot upwards. After a brief buzzing, the boy flung the door open.

"Fourth floor," he announced.

Elder had a rush of blood to his head.

"I said second floor!"

"Yes, sir."

Down they went. In a few seconds, the lift stopped. Elder made to get out, but was again halted by a wave of the boy's hand.

"Its's happened again. The door's open. Seems somebody 's having a little fun."

"Damn!"

In barely forty-five minutes Elder had succeeded in reaching his destination. He was now standing outside Room 66. The missionary's garb was hanging from its peg, and a pair of shoes were on the doorstep.

He knocked on the door.

"Who is it?" asked a hoarse voice.

"Somebody to see you, sir."

He heard the sound of slowly shuffling feet. The door was opened, and a white-haired, sallow-faced man peered out.

"You want to see me?"

"Yes, sir. Somebody down in the salon wants to see the Reverend Crawford, missionary."

"My name is Paul Sorgette."

"I am sorry. It's the Reverend Crawford they want to see."

"Well, they can't. Crawford was roasted last year at Lake Victoria Nyanza."

"Then it must be another Reverend Crawford."

"Now wait a minute. Who are you? I don't believe a word of your story. A little while ago I heard someone scratching on my door. I daresay, you look pretty suspicious to me!"

"I am Chief Inspector Elder. In any case, you'd better put the money into the strong-box."

"The what? How do you know about that?"

"The receptionist told me you'd got a money remittance. What time did you go to bed?"

"At eleven o'clock," replied the missionary and slammed the door on Elder. It was getting on to midnight.

Elder reflected for some moments, the then quickly bent down.

There was a gleam of something wet on the missionary's shoes. Liquids take long to dry on leather, but this particular liquid hadn't dried since eleven o'clock. The shoes had been bespattered with liquid when the Friday fish had been knocked to the floor. Undoubtedly, somebody must have worn the missionary's shoes while he was asleep, and the inspector know just who'd done it.

15.

Maud was taking leave of Prince Sergius outside the door of her room.

"Don't worry," she told him. "I feel there is some hope."

"I... I don't share your feeling."

"But the professor has returned today..."

"Hush! No use brooding over something that's past help. Good night."

The prince left, and Maud entered her room. She switched on the light – and found herself facing the young stranger. He was sitting in a chair with a bed sheet wrapped around his waist, but otherwise impeccably dressed in a chequered coat whose sleeves appeared a bit short.

"How dare you…"

"Quiet! I shall be brief because time is short, and besides, I'm hungry. I want you to hand me the knife and the white lace table cover you wrapped it in, and hurry. Please!"

Maud found it impossible to say anything.

"Ask no questions and spare me any explanations. Do as I say. Somebody saw you take the knife away. They're going to search your room."

"Who… Who saw me?"

"Please be quick. If they find the knife here, you're done for."

"How do I know…"

"We've no time for palavers. You've got to believe what I'm saying to you is true. If you don't, you're finished. Let me have that knife!"

She hesitated; then she quickly walked up to the window, and from a crevice next to the window-sill pulled out the white lace table cover.

"Here you are. Any other wishes?"

"None… Perhaps, if you would volunteer to tell me…"

"I'm not going to tell you anything. Think what you will. You being the murderer, I don't suppose you have reasonable grounds for holding me culpable for anything."

"What did you take this away for?"

"I'd supposed somebody else had done it, and I wanted to save him. You… You… How ever did you get here, apparelled like this?"

"It was just the crowning event of my tribulations tonight. I took the missionary's garb back to his door. Then, in a dishabille whose scantiness I have no words to describe, I made a dash for the winding stairs in an attempt to recover my pyjamas. They were nowhere to be found. I found half a dozen laundered sheets in their stead. You may well imagine my situation. So what could I do? I wrapped one of the sheets round me, and headed for this room. On the way, I saw a gentleman who was en route to his room to go to bed, supported by as many as three persons, who addressed him by the name of Vangold. They escorted this man Vangold to his room, and put him to bed. Five minutes later, they hung his clothes on the peg outside his room, and left. I borrowed the coat, but the trousers were too tight and wouldn't go on. Then I borrowed a pair of high boots from outside Room 87. I fear they belong to a police officer."

47

"How did you get to know about the knife?"

"Good night," he said, cutting her short and, grabbing his sheet just in time to keep it from slipping down, rushed out of the room.

He stopped at the corner of the passage to listen. Having established that the coast was clear, he took the dagger from his pocket and threw it out the window. Next, he went to Vangold's room, and hung the chequered coat back in its place.

He was in a hurry. He hoped he would find some sort of repository in the basement, where he would be able to hide. He felt dreadfully exhausted. He must have reached about the ground-floor level when he heard footsteps down below, and a voice called out:

"Marti-i-in, Is that you?"

Blast!

He was out in the corridor like a shot, and started for the darkened restaurant.

He heard several voices.

"Thank heaven they've opened it. Who on earth could have locked this from outside?"

"I have no idea," said the receptionist.

He turned back, and hurried past the doors. This was a perfect nightmare! He could hear some voices also at the far end of the passage.

"I thought you'd turned in, Elder."

It was Lieutenat Sedlintz, the duty officer, speaking.

"I heard some strange noise. You can't be too much on your guard at a place like this."

They were bound to arrive here in an instant. He was finding himself between the devil and the deep blue sea.

"Marti-i-i-n! You don't hear me?"

That female ought to be strangled, he thought.

He found himself right by Room 21. The Italian woman's room! A tune being hummed softly came from behind the door, followed by the soft thud of a shoe as it dropped on the floor. The voices were coming nearer.

He knocked on the door.

"Come in."

He entered Room 20, and found himself face to face with the Sicilian widow, who was dressed in a kimono, and staring at him with her mouth open.

"What are you doing here?"

"Excuse me," said the gentleman in a night shirt with a black tie, who was wrapped in a sheet that reached practically to his toes. "Since you were kind enough to invite me..."

"But you said you were keeping a fast and..."

"It's past midnight now, and Friday's become Saturday."

"I'm sorry, but... er... It's so unusual. The things you are wearing..."

"Ah, they only look strange in these parts. Actually, this is the missionary order's formal wear for leper-nursing. I donned it in your honour. White smock, dark tie and dress boots. This wear is regarded very highly throughout India."

"Isn't that remarkable? As a matter of fact, you see, I was preparing to go to bed. But never mind. Will you please just turn the other way, while I slip on some clothes."

He turned his back to her, and stood by the window. *Signora* Relli retreated behind the folding-screen to get dressed. When she emerged she was astounded to discover that the missionary had vanished from the room. It was, it seemed to her, as if he had sailed out the open window.

Which was just what he had done.

16.

Next morning the Grand Hotel awoke to a fresh sensation. Vangold, the corn dealer, had been arrested on suspicion of having murdered Dr Ranke. The black-skinned bellhop had reported that while cleaning Mr Vangold's clothes, he had found in the man's coat's pocket a blood-stained lace cover. It was the one that had disappeared from the table in the room in which Dr Ranke's dead body was found.

A deathly pale Mr Vangold was sitting before the captain.

"You'd better come clean and tell us the whole story."

"If you please," said Vangold weakly. He looked wretched and was positively whimpering. "I wish somebody would inform my wife. She's a lot brighter than I am."

"Your wife's got held up outside, and she won't be allowed to return for the duration of the quarantine."

"Oh, my god. I wish I'd gone shopping with her."

"That's immaterial to the subject. You'd better give us

a blow-by-blow account of the murder. Why did you stab Dr Ranke to death, and how did you prepare for it?"

Mr Vangold was wringing his hands.

"But, captain, surely you don't think I am a murderer."

"What about your alibi?"

"My what?"

"Your alibi. Do you have an alibi?"

The corn merchant looked frightened.

"My wife did the packing," he stuttered in alarm. "So I've no idea whether we've brought with us… a thing like that"

Now that was a bit thick, the captain thought. He was furious. Was this blighter trying to pretend to be a respectable person, innocent to the point where he didn't even know the meaning of the word alibi? What outrageous impudence!

The captain brought his fist down on the writing desk.

"Stop playing the idiot, man! I want none of your play-acting!"

"Please, captain," the accused man lamented. "I swear to you I am not play-acting. All I'm asking you to do is please call my wife right now."

He sat miserably, flanked by two police officers, feeling unhappy and wretched. The captain sat opposite him, behind the writing desk, his crossed legs stretching way back underneath it, because they were in slippers. Some scoundrel had pinched his boots from outside his door during the night. It was most painful.

"The murder was committed while the announcement was being made about the quarantine. Where were you during that time? Eh?"

"Why, I was speaking with you!"

"Mm. Yes… I remember that. You enquired about how strong the military cordon was."

"I am innocent, I swear to you."

"Do you mean to say that you stayed in the foyer all the time?"

Vangold said nothing.

"Well? Before you spoke with me, had you been among the other guests? I warn you that I will question every single person you may claim was standing next to you. Come on, man, make a clean breast of it and lessen the burden of your plight."

"But I *was* there!"

"Where? Come on, tell me. Do you have an alibi or don't you?"

"I repeat I don't know about that. It's my wife who always does the shopping, and…"

"I warn you for the last time: Stop playing the idiot!"

"I swear to you I'm not playing," Vangold said, whining, and fumbled about his deathly pale face with trembling fingers.

"Where had you been before you spoke with me?"

"With a lady… a Mrs Villiers…"

There came a knock on the door, and Chief Inspector Elder entered.

"Sorry to disturb you people," he said. "I want to make a report."

"You can do that when we've finished questioning the subject," the captain said.

Elder sat down. He drew astonished looks when he said, apologetically: "Permit me to be a silent witness at this questioning. It's part of my brief anyway to interview each guest in connection with the case I am investigating."

"Well, Mr Vangold," the captain said sternly, resuming his questioning. "What did you discuss with Mrs Villiers?"

Vangold moaned, wringing his hands.

"Mrs Villiers stopped by the window, and I said it was a nice day… Later on, I introduced myself and then…"

Vangold mopped his brow.

"Go on."

"She asked me to come into her room for a moment. It's on the ground floor."

"Yes?"

"In her room she placed some sandwiches before me… Small salted cheese sandwiches they were. The sort they sell in boxes. Packs sealed with lead as if it was perishable food."

"Nonsense!"

"Of course it is. After all, crackers keep well, but they sell more readily when…"

The captain banged the table.

"What happened in Mrs Villers's room?"

"I made a phone call."

"Whom to?"

"I… I don't know."

The captain heaved a deep sigh, then lit a cigarette.

"Smoke?" he said to the squirming criminal. If the man could be made to calm down and relax, he told himself, then he might be able to get him to deliver the goods.

"They contain no opium, I hope. My wife says it's harmful stuff."

"No, they don't contain any opium." He gave Vangold a light, and then leaned back in his chair. "Whom did you call on the phone? I am now applying my softest approach," he said with the amiability of a tiger tamer.

"Mrs Villiers dialled the number, and... applying various... promptings and encouragements... she persuaded me to say to the man on the other end the following: 'Arthur is onto you'."

"And did you?"

"Er... Yes. Mrs Villiers instantly pressed the rest, so I didn't hear the reply."

"Which room did all that happen in?"

"Number 42. That's the room Mrs Villiers occupies."

"We will question Mrs Villiers. Gorck, go and ask Mrs Villiers to come here, will you."

"I swear to you, captain, I am innocent," Vangold moaned.

"How did the blood-stained white lace table cover come to be in your coat pocket? It's obvious that the blade was wiped in it."

"I've no idea. You see, I was under the influence of drink, sort of, what with me having the blues on account of my wife being absent."

"I am sorry, but that blood-stained cover is conclusive proof. No jury in the world would let a man off after the blood-stained object with which the crime was committed had been found in a piece of clothing he'd been wearing."

Elder leaped to his feet.

"In this event we are facing a sensational new twist in the case," he exclaimed. "I have found the blood-stained dagger in a dress-boot. If we find the man whose dress-boots are missing, we'll have the other guilty party as well. A double of the blood-stained object has been found tucked into his footwear!"

The captain's jaw dropped, and, without being aware of it, he pulled his feet under his seat.

17.

"What's it you said?" the captain asked Elder after regaining his composure.

"If we accept the blood-stained object as irrefutable evidence of guilt, then the owner of that boot must be an accomplice of Mr Vangold's."

"Where was that boot found?"

"Outside Room 87."

"That's *my* room!" the captain exclaimed.

"The boots may have been placed there later. Captain Dickman is an early riser, and the bellhop found the boot just a little while ago."

"The... er... boot belongs to me, too."

At this, silence fell.

"In this event," Vangold exclaimed, "there's no jury anywhere in the world that would acquit Captain Dickman."

"Rubbish! My boots were outside my door. Somebody took them away, and placed the knife in one of them."

"There, you see. My coat, too, was hanging outside *my* door, and somebody came and took it away, and stuffed the lace cover into the pocket. Now you people either let me go free at once or else detain Captain Dickman as well!"

This was an awkward situation, to be sure.

"Now, Mr Vangold. I didn't detain you. I just caused you to be brought here for questioning."

"I am going to report this incident at my embassy. I'll insist on full apology being given to me and I will demand a reparation."

"Chief Inspector Elder ought to have reported this development sooner."

"I was about to make my report, sir, but you told me to wait until you've done with the questioning, sir. Orders have to be obeyed."

"I am suspending your questioning, Mr Vangold, but I may want to have another talk with you, so you must make yourself available to us."

"I shall report this at the Admiralty also!" the corn dealer cried in agitation, and rushed off.

"Bellhop just stopped me," said Elder. "He said he'd seen a pair of boots in front of Room 87. He took them away, and as he picked them up, this thing dropped out of one of the pair."

He produced a dagger from his pocket, and placed it before Captain Dickman. It was a short pointed hunting-knife sort of thing with a black hilt, and it was wrought in a slightly antique style. Engraved in its jewel-studded grip was the Roman numeral for 2. The dagger was marvellously lightweight, and there were iron stains on its blade.

"There is little doubt that this was the murder weapon," the captain remarked. "Markheit performed the autopsy this morning. He found a short wound with a wide slit where the blade had entered the body. This blade is a short one, but thick and broad underneath the hilt."

"But why is it so light?" one of the officers, fiddling with the dagger, asked. "This is like a toy."

"In fact it is," said the captain. "It isn't a real weapon. It is a trinket or a toy. Had the stab hit a bone, the blade would have been either bent or broken. But who on earth may have borrowed my boots?"

"If my theory holds water, Vangold used a brilliant ploy, provided it was him who put the dagger into your boot, sir," one of the policemen hazarded.

"That's a good theory," Elder said approvingly. "Although, considering that last night a missionary's garb was also stolen and later returned..."

The police officers looked embarrassed.

"By the way, what kind of a case are you investigating, Chief Inspector?" the captain asked.

"I am hunting a criminal, and the clues led here. They made me promise that I would divulge nothing about the persons involved."

"I s'pose that doesn't go for your superiors?"

"I should think not. If you will ring up Chief Counsellor Meulen, sir, I trust he will relieve me of the duty of non-disclosure of an official secret."

"Thank you," Captain Dickman said icily. "I think the two cases can be handled separately."

The officer who had been sent to fetch Mrs Villiers returned. With him came Counsellor Markheit.

"I beg to report, sir, that Mrs Villiers has disappeared from the hotel," the lieutenant reported.

"What!"

"I knocked on the doors of all the rooms in the hotel. Counsellor Markheit here dispatched the medical corps people all over the place, and the search has established beyond any doubt that Mrs Villiers is not to be found in the hotel."

"Who is the last person who saw her?" the captain asked.

"It's the waiter, sir. The one who served breakfast to Mrs Villiers in the garden. The man also noted that the vanished person later took a walk in the garden, and talked with the sentry who is posted at the barbed-wire checkpoint outside the entrance gate."

The captain looked at Markheit in puzzlement.

"Is it possible for anyone to get through the cordon?"

"Well... That is something that's happened before, you see. But It's extremely difficult." He turned to face the slighted chief inspector. "What do *you* think, Elder?"

Elder looked at the captain. "I have no objection to your replying to Counsellor Markheit," the captain said in embarrassment. "If anyone here can have an opinion at all."

"First thing I should question the sentry Mrs Villiers was seen talking with. And the waiter too."

Markheit snapped his fingers.

"By George! You sure have hit the nail on the head. Don't you think so, captain?"

"Of course the questioning of those two persons must go ahead without fail. This would have been done anyway. Now, Mr Sedlintz, will you please send for the waiter and that soldier." He turned to Markheit. "I don't expect the questionings will turn up too much information, though," he said.

The waiter didn't say anything that was new. He had served breakfast to Mrs Villiers at nine o'clock.

"Did she appear nervous or agitated?"

The waiter shrugged his shoulders.

"That lady is slightly edgy all the time... That time she appeared relatively composed. She read a newspaper and wrote a letter."

"Did you see her go back into the lounge after breakfast?"

"No, sir. She was talking with the sentry, and I had to go into the kitchen again and when I came back she was nowhere to be seen."

"Thank you. You may go."

The sentry came: he had gone off duty – and become another captive at the Grand Hotel for the duration of the quarantine.

"You were seen talking with a certain lady this morning."

"Yes, sir. We're under orders not be unfriendly to people staying at this place. We are allowed to chat with them even when on sentry duty and are accosted by a guest from across the fence."

"What did you and that lady talk about?"

"She asked me what time I was going to be stood down... And wanted to know if it was all right for me to accept any gifts. I told her we weren't permitted to, as various objects might spread the disease."

"Did you see her again later on?"

"I did not, sir."

"You may go."

"Wait!" Elder cut in. He walked up to the medic.

"Look, my friend. If you surrender that letter now, it'll mean for you two days in the dark-cell. But if you don't, I'll take the view that you attempted to smuggle it out. And that's a case for a court-martial."

"But... Please, sir... I..."

"Stop stuttering or I'll crush your bloody bones for you!" Elder yelled. "That woman told you she'd pay you to smuggle a letter out of here! And that's what you did yesterday. You committed an act of..."

"I didn't do that, sir. She came to see me about it for the first time today..."

"Unhand that letter, and you'll get away with it."

Deathly pale, the sentry produced an envelope from his pocket.

"What did she tell you?" the chief inspector kept on badgering him.

"She said she'd give me... a hundred guilders.. if I'd smuggle this letter out... I didn't want to... But she cried, she implored me..."

"Get out of my sight! You are being kept in quarantine! I'll decide later on what I'll say about you in my report."

The sentry left the room.

"It was practically a cinch," Elder explained. "Why does anyone write a letter here when it can't be posted for three weeks? To have it smuggled out, of course. The simplest way to do that is to make a beeline for the sentry and see him about it."

"May I take a look at that letter?" the captain said quietly.

Elder handed it to him.

The envelope was addressed to a Mr Arthur Brocklin, in Singapore.

"I think we have reason enough to tear this open," said the captain, sounding undecided, but opened it right away.

The letter said:

"*I want you to know the truth. Marjorie and Doddy have met. They are staying together at the Grand Hotel on Little Lagonda, and are trapped in quarantine here. That Italian woman, Signora Relli, knew about that business, too. They are making fun of you…*"

There was no signature.

"This business is getting tangled more and more," said the captain, toying with the dagger.

"What do *you* think, Elder?" Markheit said.

"We ought to see this *Signora* Relli, sir."

"Why, of course," said the captain. "Mr Sedlintz, will you please send for *Signora* Relli."

She turned up, looking provocative in a dress of black silk, with eyes shining and clear as of someone who had had a good night's sleep. The whiff of a light perfume wafted into the room as she entered. She was smiling and greeted those present loudly.

"Good morning, gentlemen. You have made poor Mr Vangold rather miserable."

"He is a bit touchy. All we did was to ask of him a few pieces of information. Pray, be seated, *Signora*."

"Thank you."

She kept twisting a sumptuous string of large pearls around a forefinger.

"Do you know a Mr Arthur Brocklin?"

She reflected, pursing her lips.

"Brocklin?… It's a fairly common name, but I'm afraid I don't know anyone by that name… Is it anything to do with poor Dr Ranke's case?"

"At first we believed so," the captain said. "However, in the meantime several other mysterious affairs have come to our attention."

Captain Dickman picked up the dagger, and toyed with it nervously.

"What is that?" *Signora* Relli asked, craning her neck.

"This is a dagger. It is a toy, but it made a handy weapon to kill Dr Ranke with," he said, and held it out for her.

Signora Relli slumped to the floor in a faint.

18.

Having jumped into the garden, the bed sheet-clad young man warily crept along the wall. He nearly dropped with exhaustion.

Glancing up, he saw above him an open window of frosted glass. It would not be a residential room, he surmised, but a room with wash-basins or showers. He made his bed sheet into a roll, tied it around his waist, and then climbed up to the windowsill. Inside, there was darkness and silence.

He quietly slipped into the room. He was sure it was untenanted. His hand touched a bath-tub. He was chary of moving about, as he saw a chink of light under the door. Presently, his hand touched some sort of covering cloth; he felt it and found that it reached almost to the floor. Just the thing! It must be a bench of sorts for the bathing guest, he figured. He hoped no one would come and have a bath early in the morning, so he quickly lifted the cover and crept under the bench, and presently fell asleep.

He woke to the realisation that Dr Ranke's dead body was being dissected overhead.

It was morning, full and clear. What he had taken to be a bench turned out to be a dissection-table. Had he stretched out a hand a little bit farther in the night he would have touched the cadaver.

"The liver is slightly swollen. Traces of recurrent malaria… No, don't write that down, my friend," said a voice he recognized as being that of Markheit. "Swollen lymphatic tissue the size of a pea on inner wall of stomach. Resembles healed ulcer. Right… Let's go on… I say, what time d'you make it? I'm getting quite hungry… That's nothing… All right. Now go on writing. Discoloration of about an inch around opening of stab-wound that starts from outer lobe of lung. Contused surface, presumably from handle of dagger… Phew! Is it hot in here!… There… That's nothing… All right, we can go now." He dictated amid the rustling sound of a smock. "Cause of death: rapid haemorrhage resulting from severed artery along stab-wound… Gruber, you sew this up. I want the report typed, two copies, and brought to me to the lunch table."

The man named Gruber started pottering away with the sewing, the waxed thread from time to time giving off a rustling noise. The other people washed their hands, then left the room.

From his hideout under the cover, Felix could see shoes moving away.

One shoe was made of white tennis webbing, rather soiled, and with an odd-shaped brown coffee stain on it!

The wearer of that shoe was the person who brought the letter into Maud's room. He now reached the doorstep. Damn this Gruber fellow! If he didn't stay behind to do this blasted sewing job, he could have found out now.

Well, that chance was lost.

The door was closed. They were gone, and this Gruber twerp had stayed behind to do his damned sewing. And the rotter was humming a song over it, no less!

"Gosh," Felix thought, was it hot here, under the table! The air was stuffy. "Now let me see," he considered. "Who could have attended the autopsy? Chief Medical Counsellor Markheit, his surgeons and assistant surgeons. In general, nobody but surgeons." It followed that the white shoe with the brown stain was worn by a surgeon.

The heat was getting unbearable. "This blighter is taking an unconscionable time sewing up that thing," he fumed. And singing softly to himself the while, the stinker is!

At last! The man Gruber was scrubbing up – and he was whistling a tune! This cad was making a joke of this sordid business! Having great fun, he was!

But Gruber was leaving at last, and Hunted Game Felix was free to crawl out from under the dissection table and breathe more freely. The corpse, stretched out on the table, was covered. This was a loathsome place. How on earth could you get out of this dissecting-room alive if you weren't a surgeon? He took a look round, and saw several smocks hung on the wall. He quickly put on one of them, an ankle-length smock. He walked to the door like grim Death, resolved to leave the room, come what might. Boot ankles clicked: the sentry saluted him. Splendid. He hadn't noticed anything amiss.

"Which way did the colleagues go?" he asked the man.

"The disinfection chamber's been installed in the basement, sir."

"Thank you."

They were in the ground floor annex corridor. Dressing-rooms, power-room, lumber-rooms, closets. He hurried off.

Felix reached the hotel corridor, emerged into it, and walked on its carpet-covered floor. Where was he headed? He wished he knew.

"I say, doctor."

He had been addressed by a hulking fattish man, who was standing in an open door.

"Yes?"

"My name is Johannes Bruns. I thought Dr Markheit had sent you to see me."

"Yes... Oh, yes... I passed your room."

"Won't you come inside,"

Felix entered quickly. It occurred to him that in this room, perhaps, he might lay his hands on some sort of clothing.

"Well now. What is the matter?"

The giant was a broad-shouldered man with coarse features and flashy clothes. He looked at his white-smocked visitor with a woefully suffering mien.

"Dr Markheit said you would be able to help me, doctor. After all, you're the great Professor Raleigh's son."

"That's right. I am John Raleigh. What's the trouble?"

"Isn't your name Charles?"

"Why, of course. My name is John Charles Raleigh. I'm called John after my grandfather. I use this first name. Well now, What is your complaint?"

"Didn't Dr Markheit tell you?"

"He did. Sure... By and large... He gave me a broad outline... A rough idea, you know... However, one had better get it from the horse's mouth. I mean, having the patient tell it himself... Well, how long have you had these aches?"

"Me? I have no aches whatsoever."

"I meant to say this catarrh... That is to say, this fever... When did it begin? Oh, it's hot in here." He mopped his brow.

"I've never had any fever, nor catarrh," said the patient in amazement. "I don't get this."

"Ah well, what I mean is, I expected you would have these symptoms, because whenever you get headaches..."

"I never do."

What the hell could this bloke be suffering from?

"I never have headaches," the man repeated.

"Indeed? Now that gives cause for alarm. With a case of rheumatism."

"I haven't got rheumatism,"

This was just about hopeless.

"Well then, what *ails* you?"

"Nothing."

"Oh. Now, we'll take care of that. Ever take medicines?"

"Never," Bruns sighed. Sweat of mortal fear shone on his worn and haggard face. "I think nothing can help, except Lee Shing."

"Er... A Chinese internist, I presume."

"No. My illness is called Lee Shing. Dr Markheit said he'd discuss this business with you."

"Of course... We did discuss it... However, one wants to hear what the patient has to say."

Hey, what was this? A well-laid table. Refreshments, delicious cold snacks. Something seldom seen in a gravely ill patient's room – and the sight of it all caused excruciating pain to the gentleman named Felix, who for the past twenty-four hours hadn't had any food, having spent the time being on the run, rushing about, dressing and undressing and attending an autopsy... What a perfect tenderloin steak!

"It all began four years ago," the man with the coarse features and the hulking figure of a butcher said, sighing deeply. He was gaudily dressed and had large flat hands like a pair of baking pans. "It happened four years ago. I went to Kuala Lumpur for the first time. It all began there, one clammy and hot evening."

"The shivering-fit?"

"No. Love."

"Six of one, half a dozen of the other."

"I met Lee Shing, and we fell in love with each other. Oh, how I loved her. But, you know, a Chinese woman, and that evil-smelling, overcrowded place. Kuala Lumpur... In short, after two months I put an end to the affair. Secretly, during the night, I boarded a ship and sailed away. Far away, to Shanghai. That's where it all began. Five minutes after I had landed, an Old Chinese showed up to see me. 'Lee Shing sent this message, sir', he said, and handed me a letter. Lee Shing had dictated it to some Chinese rascal. In it she said she was withdrawing to some place, taking to the woods somewhere, and there she would keep running her mind night and day over a curse that would make me die. When the time came, I should remember Lee Shing for the last time: she would send me four mimosa flowers announcing the approach of death. When I'd have received the fourth flower

I should be prepared to face death... You're smiling. I smiled, too, and I booted out that old Chinese. And yet I'd heard say a good deal about that superstition, and here, in the East seen a man so cursed keep on losing flesh daily and waste away, and no doctor was able to cure him. Three months ago I received the first flower, and it would have made me laugh, had it not happened in London."

"What!"

"Yes, sir. In the bathroom of my London flat, a mimosa flower lay on the floor, and no one could tell me how it had come to be there. Next, I came down with flu. I was seriously ill. And since that time, my materialistic bias has been shaken. I began to be haunted by fear. I've had bad dreams. I began losing weight."

"How much had you weighed before you started losing weight?"

"Over two hundred pounds," the man replied with a woeful sigh, and lit himself a cigarette. "Then I started to look for Lee Shing, but she had disappeared from Kuala Lumpur. I spent thousands of pounds sterling, hiring lots of people in my quest to search for her all over Asia. It was no use. Then in Colombo, two months ago, on my breakfast table one morning, I found the second mimosa."

"May I ask you," said the white-smocked man, "what is your job, actually?"

The stout fellow shot a fleeting glance around the room. "I'm a person of independent means."

Painful silence fell. It was obvious that he was telling a lie. The hunted young man cast a yearning glance at the small table that was laden with the food.

"Then," the stout one went on, "yesterday the disaster happened."

"Yet another mimosa?"

"Precisely."

He wiped his brow, which was bathed in sweat from terror. This man was really in serious trouble. His yellowish skin and the dim look in his eyes were stamped with the message of death.

"Dr Markheit said he would send you to see me, Dr Raleigh. He said you'd successfully cured a ship's officer who was similarly affected."

"Yes. Yes, indeed... A pretty good case, it was."

"It was just like mine?"

"No. That one had daffodils sent to him. But he too was losing weight."

"Well, doctor, I've lost all hope... I've no appetite, my muscles have become flaccid, I'm short of breath. But the worst part of it is my loss of appetite. I find it impossible to eat."

"That beats me," Felix said, breathing heavily, and swallowing painfully.

"There's food on that table all day long. I hoped it might whet my appetite. It's no go... I wonder... Did your ship's officer have the same problem?"

The young man brightened up like magic.

"The very same. That was precisely the point where I achieved success."

"How?"

"By means of hypnotic suggestion. That is the only way. You will be cured under the influence of a will stronger than your own."

"Really?... Say, you will not be sorry if you can do that... I despaired when Dr Markheit said you'd be able to come and see me only if..." he winced "there was no autopsy. For me, this is of the utmost urgency, otherwise, I'm done for."

The smock-clad man felt relieved. It was perfectly safe. The doctor named Raleigh would not come and see this man because the autopsy took place this morning.

"Now, if you please... We will begin the hypnotic suggestion. You must copy everything I shall be doing, no matter how difficult you should find it to do so. Do what I tell you. I cured the ship's officer of the same sort of insanity fifteen minutes before his death... Get up... There... Look me in the eye. Look hard... Come... Sit down... There..."

They were sitting at the table. His nostrils dilating, the young man cut into the meat and, staring the terrified-looking Bruns in the eyes, said:

"Cut off a slice of meat! Good... Now put it into your mouth." He began to eat greedily. "Fine... Now chew it!... Chew!... Fine... Again!" He cut off another slice and ate it. His eyes were shining. The other man was following his example with utmost difficulty, a childishly weepy look on his beefy face. "Go on eating... Attaboy!... A delicious example like this is infectious... Same thing happened to that seafaring fellow... Eat... Chew! CHEW! Look me in the eye! Chew! Eat! Got any mustard?"

The patient looked at his healer flabbergasted. In the course of the doctor's hypnotic suggestion therapy, all of the food disappeared from the table in a flash.

Eventually, however, the sight of the man stuffing food into his mouth put Bruns into the mood, and he started eating. This man was a damn good doctor, he thought.

"Now you pour yourself some of this whisky."

"I can't."

"I won't take no for an answer. Do as I do, and drink!" And he drank. He finally got to drink!

Bruns drained his glass of whisky.

"What now?" he asked.

"Now you will join me in singing 'It's a long way to Tipperary' ten times. There's a nice chap."

A little while later, the missionary next door beat on the wall with both hands, yelling that they should stop this unendurable caterwauling, or he'll go see the manager about this. But the two men ignored the cleric's protest completely; indeed, the rollicking twosome broke into a dance. Before long they were dancing reels with a verve and vivacity that made the windowpanes rattle.

19.

When Signora Relli came to, she said nothing about what had caused her to faint.

"This often happens to me during the rainy season. Just two days ago I wanted to leave here and go to the hills," she said.

"However, the sight of the dagger..." the captained suggested.

"I resent this insinuation," the *Signora* countered.

"It's nothing of the kind. I thought it reminded you of something."

"It was a terrible sigh. And this season, too, is absolutely terrible. This quarantine business may cost me my life if I cannot go to the hills very soon."

The captain threw Elder a quizzical look. The chief inspector picked up the dagger.

"Indeed, this is nothing particular to look at. Could you tell me, *Signora*, why this object is so light?"

"How should I know? Maybe it's a toy."

"Have you any idea of what the Roman numeral two here stands for?"

"Maybe it's the price tag."

Elder nodded.

"Possibly. Though prices are customarily marked in Arabic numerals. I would rather say it's some sort of a sign."

The *Signora* was nervously toying with her pearls.

"I have no idea," she said quickly. "I may now go, I believe."

"Yes, of course. Still, may I trouble you for a moment?" said Elder, smiling.

"Are you empowered to carry out interrogations? To the best of my knowledge, that comes within the Captain's authority."

Elder kept nodding in appreciation.

"A happy guess, *Signora*. I hope Captain Vuyder will ask you how you came to know what's in the service cards issued by the Central Police Station."

She rose, white-faced.

"Arrest me if you dare. But I will not put up with you humiliating and badgering me with questions!"

"We asked you a civil question, *Signora*. Your nervousness is perplexing."

She sat down again.

"*Si*. All right, go ahead and ask your questions. But this gentleman is wearing civilian clothes."

"Chief Inspector Edler is a renowned policeman, and I asked him to take charge of the investigation," said the captain, and he blushed because he was aware that he was capitulating.

"Frankly," Elder said, turning to face her, "I don't see why you should be angry with me, *Signora*. I am a staunch admirer of yours, and by no means would I involve you in this case. All I wish to do is put a few questions to you."

"*Va bene*. Please yourself. I know nothing about the dagger."

"But my dear *Signora*," said Elder, smiling. "Who is talking of the dagger? What I would like to know is this. When did *Signor* Relli die?"

"Is that really important?"

"It's an established custom to take down people's particulars."

"My husband died eight years ago."

"What of?"

"Is that, too, anything to do with my identity?"

"By no means. I'd just like to know."

"Oh, really. Well, Arnoldo died eight years ago."

"And where is he buried?"

"In Vicenza, Italy. Would you please tell me what business that is of yours?"

Captain Vuyder looked at Elder in a strange sort of way.

"Is that really important, Elder?"

"If it isn't, then why does it make *Signora* Relli so nervous?"

"Because I am offended by strangers poking their noses into my private affairs."

"In that case I desist," the chief inspector said graciously. "I would only ask you to please tell me the meaning of this number two on the dagger."

The Signora sprang to her feet, her lips trembling.

"I've told you, I don't know. It must be a toy dagger. Something for children to play with."

Elder planted himself squarely in front of her, and looked her in the eyes.

"You're wrong, *Signora* Manzini. This is a toy for grown-ups."

At first, the Signora appeared taken aback. Then she shrugged, and whispered dejectedly:

"*Sì*. You know everything. I admit I am Nedda Manzini."

Her admission caused raised eyebrows all round. The captain drew a hand across his forehead.

"I seem to have heard that name somewhere."

"Of course you have. There was a time when that was a household name the world over. I was once an opera singer. That was eighteen years ago. Then I quit the stage and followed a missionary as far afield as Borneo... And when he died..." At this, tears welled up in her eyes. "... I resolved that I should return to Italy. But I hate the prospect of being an old artiste, so I became instead a young widow, and assumed the name of Relli. It's detestable when people feel sorry for you on account of your past greatness. That is how I became *Signora* Relli. *Basta*. I hope I've satisfied your curiosity."

"Ah, it was nothing of the sort. I just wanted to know how many artistes there are in this hotel."

Markheit shook his head in disapproval. What was this fellow driving at again, he wondered.

"What do you want to know that for?" she inquired nervously.

"Because this dagger is stage property," Elder said.

Silence fell.

"And just what do you mean by that?"

"I mean to say that he wants to know each artiste in this building who may be assumed to have put away a prop somewhere as a souvenir." He looked at the dagger. "A prop which was used in Act Two of an opera."

"Are you suspecting me?"

"No. But when I find a dagger that was once a stage property, then I must know whether there are in this building artistes other than Mr Lindner."

"Lindner is a simple soul, an honest gentleman."

"Nobody says he is a suspect. We will just question him in connection with the dagger. Lieutenant Sedlintz is going to ask him to come here," Elder said, issuing directives.

"Please, gentlemen, I beg you. It's absolutely certain that he has nothing to do with the dagger."

"Calm yourself, *Signora*."

"No! Lindner has a heart ailment, he is a bad case of nerves, and so chicken-hearted... You will kill him."

She was wringing her hands. The police officers grew more and more astonished. Was this Elder fellow a sorcerer? Where on earth had he got hold of the startling facts he was producing?

"You can trust us to proceed with tact, *Signora*. And now, while we'll be questioning Mr Lindner, will you please retire to the office. Lieutenant Borgen will keep you company."

"All right. I feel sorry for that big child. I'm fond of him, too. But, believe me, he has nothing to do with this whole business. You mustn't hold him under suspicion. Please be careful!" She was almost in tears in her entreaty. "He badly needs to be taken care of."

She went over into the third room, accompanied by Lieutenant Borgen.

"I say, how did you find out all that about this case?" Captain Vuyder inquired of Elder.

"Remember I'd started my investigation half a day before you people. This Italian woman was familiar to me. So I cabled to the consulate, and they gave me a run-down on her. The authorities are well aware of her secret. Will really put me in charge of the investigations, Captain Vuyder?"

"Yes. I admit my opinion of you has changed. I supposed that you owed more to your good luck than to your capabilities."

"The two must go hand in hand to be worth anything."

Lieutenant Sedlintz came back, escorting the fat, baby-faced singer. The latter had bags under his eyes, loose dark areas of skin that had formed over the years, and in the fat around his jawbone the passage of time had deepened a hollow that looked like side-whiskers. He was breathing with difficulty, and his lids would slide drowsily over a pair of yellowish, bloodshot eyes.

"Have a seat, Mr Lindner."

"Thank you," he said and sat down, huffing and puffing. Captain Vuyder was about to produce the dagger, but found that it had disappeared from the table. Where on earth was it?

"Yes."

"But before he finished reading it, you had left the foyer."

"That's right. I went up to my room because I felt tired and didn't give a damn for the whole business."

"It is a tedious business, no doubt. You didn't come across somebody in the corridor, by any chance?"

"Prince Sergius. He was coming from the direction of my room. We exchanged greetings."

"Anybody else?"

"I saw a young lady who occupies a room on the same floor. She appeared to be waiting for the prince."

"It was Miss Maud Borckman. You went into your room?"

"No. *Signora* Relli unexpectedly called out to me."

"But she was downstairs, in the foyer!"

"Indeed. But meanwhile she had gone upstairs. She had taken the elevator, and when I reached the floor, I found her there. She asked me to go and fetch her handbag. She had left it in the foyer, and she said she had a lot of money in it."

"And you went downstairs and fetched it for her?"

"I didn't find it in the foyer. It really beats me."

"Thank you," Elder said. "That's all there's been to the formalities."

"Fine. Glad to be of service." He rose to his feet with some difficulty.

"By the by, we can attend to this request of Mr Wolfgang's," Elder shot at him, smiling. "This trinket was found in the waste paper basket, and we don't know who it belongs to."

He produced the dagger from his pocket. Lindner's muffin face brightened.

"It's mine. It's a nice souvenir. It was used in Act Two of *The Marksman*. My finest role was in that particular opera."

"How could it have ended up in the waste paper basket?"

"It may have dropped from my writing-desk. I always had it there."

"You will have to claim it from the manager's office. That too is mere formality. We aren't authorized to hand over lost property. Just one thing more. Did you notice a striking brownish stain on your carpet?"

The door of the adjoining room was flung open, and an excited *Signora* Relli emerged from behind it.

"Stop that!"

Lindner got up, amazed.

"I want to make a confession."

"But, *Signora*..."

"I want Mr Lindner to leave this room. It's all right. You've nothing to be afraid of. We've got to settle a misunderstanding."

"I am not going to leave this room. I want to know what's going on here. What's the meaning of all this?"

Elder lit a cigarette.

"Please be seated, Mr Lindner. You too, *Signora*. *S'accomodi*."

She sat down, slightly surprised to hear the Italian word.

"I think we'd better get everything straight right now. We are holding neither of you under suspicion, and it won't do any harm to Mr Lindner either to learn the truth. If you please, *Signora*. Go ahead and tell us."

By now she appeared far more composed.

"When Captain Vuyder started reading out the order imposing the quarantine, I saw Mr Lindner start climbing the stairs. He was walking at a somewhat unsteady tread. I wanted to stop him having any more drinks. It had been a day full of confusion anyway. I took the elevator and rode up in order to be at his room ahead of him. When I got there I saw that the door was ajar, and inside, a man's dead body was lying in a pool of blood."

Lindner was listening, transfixed.

"It was Dr Ranke," Elder said.

"*Si*. It was his body. I knew that all the guests were downstairs in the foyer."

"There you were mistaken."

"I believed that Lindner was the only person who had come

upstairs. I realized that he had no alibi because he'd left the foyer. You see, I am a cool-headed, strong woman. I used to live with a missionary in Borneo. Across the corridor was a door half open, with a broom leaned against the wall: they were just doing the room. It was Vangold's room, and he did have an alibi. I picked up the body and heaved it... I am a muscular woman... and quickly carried it into the other room. I heard voices outside, and went to the door. Somebody opened it, but it concealed me completely. When that person saw the dead man, he or she slammed the door shut and walked away. I too left. I didn't have the courage to pull the dagger out from Dr Ranke's body. In the corridor I ran into Lindner. I told him to go downstairs to the foyer. I thought maybe nobody had seen him leave in the first place. Then I rushed to my room."

"All this while did you run into anyone else?"

"Well... I saw Maud Borckman saying goodbye to Prince Sergius. They were standing on the staircase."

"I was quite sure," Elder said, "that Dr Ranke hadn't been murdered on the spot where they found his body. There was scarcely any blood on the floor, and the autopsy report says the cause of the death was mortal haemorrhage. I was looking for the blood."

Lindner rose.

"Gentlemen, I must make a confession. It was I who killed Dr Ranke."

The widow sprang to her feet, but this time the captain called out to her sharply.

"Please, *Signora*. This is an interrogation. You're not supposed to speak unless you're asked a question."

Already he was cleverly bypassing Elder. He moved quickly just as things appeared to have entered the home straight. In the space of half an hour, the chief inspector had inexorably elbowed everyone else from this case. Oho! This fellow was a fast operator. He needed to be reined in.

"Your name?" asked the captain.

"Enrico Lindner."

Sedlintz had lots of time in front of him.

"Lindner isn't an Italian name."

"My father was Austrian. I was born Italian in 1886, in Turin."

The languid, uneasy man was now calm, cool and level-headed.

"Are you going to make a full admission of your guilt?" the captain asked.

"Yes, sir. I admit to having murdered Dr Ranke in my room."

"How did it happen?"

"Dr Ranke knocked on my door and said the police had arrived, and would I please come down to the foyer. I opened the door, the doctor entered, and was surprised to find *me* in occupancy. He had believed the room was still occupied by the lady I had exchanged rooms with."

Elder sprang to his feet.

"What! Was it not you who occupied that room?"

"No. I'd taken Room 72, and the receptionist had asked me to give it up to a lady."

"Any idea who that lady was?"

"Maud Borckman," Elder said.

"Go on."

"The doctor asked me the number of the room that lady had moved in to. I was annoyed by the way he fired his questions at me, rapidly, impatiently, so I gave a negative answer. At that he grabbed my arm, and started yelling at me. I shoved him, and he hit me. I snatched up the stage dagger, which was at hand, and stabbed him."

"Why did you go down to the foyer after you had stabbed him?"

"Once again, there came a knock on the door. This time it was the detective, who said I should go to the foyer, as the police were there. I was afraid that he might come in, so I went downstairs with him, but came back upstairs right away to remove the body. But *Signora* Relli sent me to fetch her hand-bag. By the time I came back, the body had disappeared."

"What about the carpet?" Elder inquired.

"Pardon?" said Lindner, gazing stupidly.

"The blood stained carpet. Where had it gone? With your subsequent approval, I entered your room yesterday, and found it was the only one on the same floor in which the carpet was missing."

"Indeed! Now you mention it, it seems off to me, too. That carpet's gone!"

"I don't see the importance of this point," the captain cut in impatiently.

"In my view it is of considerable importance," Elder retorted.

"The victim's blood still hasn't been found. It ran onto that carpet, if you ask me."

"How can it have vanished, over the murderer's head so to speak," the captain said impatiently. "No one but he could have wanted to make it disappear,"

Elder leaned back in his chair, whistling noiselessly.

"Well?" one of the officers prompted him nervously.

"The carpet is of utmost importance in the whole affair." He turned suddenly towards Lindner. "What position were the two of you standing in when you stabbed the doctor in the stomach?"

"We were standing face to face, and I stuck it straight into his belly." Lindner stopped in astonishment. He could see from the dumbfounded faces around him that something extraordinary must have happened.

"All right," Elder said and stood up. "This matter is now beginning to clear up. You've given yourself away, Mr Lindner. Dr Ranke was not stabbed in the belly. The dagger was plunged into his throat."

Lindner nervously ran his fingers through his thinning hair.

"I didn't hear the question right. Of course I plunged the dagger into his throat. He was facing me, and I wanted to hit a soft point with this light instrument. So I aimed at his throat."

He broke off in alarm as Signora Relli burst out laughing. She laughed lustily. It was a hearty, full-throated laughter; it came from a person who looked relieved and cheerful.

20.

"*Signor* Elder! *Benissimo*! You are a devil and an angel rolled into one," the *Signora* exclaimed, and before anyone could have prevented her, quickly bowed down and kissed the chief inspector's hand.

"But, *Signora*…"

"Don't speak." She walked up to Lindner. "Oh, you terrible, foolish child of a man! For shame! You frightened me so. I should never have thought you had such capability of telling lies. Shame on you."

The old fat child sat down, completely crushed.

"It was I who killed him," he mumbled.

"*Basta*! You silly man. Dr Ranke was stabbed from behind, and stabbed in the throat, not in the belly!"

"What does all this mean, Elder?"

"It means that it is the carpet that matters. Who removed the carpet, and why? The blood stain was on the carpet."

"But..."

"As for Mr Lindner, I believe part of his confession is true. Dr Ranke had been looking for Maud Borckman, unaware that she had moved out from Mr Lindner's room. Mr Lindner told him she had occupied another room, and..."

"Yes?" said the captain encouragingly.

"Answer the question, Mr Lindner," Elder said to the singer. "Every word matters."

Once again, the singer was his old, helpless self.

"I lied to you people just now. I believed the *Signora* might fall under suspicion. I thought I'd better shoulder it."

"You foolish old child!" the Signora cried.

"Quiet, please," the captain interjected. "As I take it, you wish to alter your confession,"

"Yes, I do."

"What happened between you and Dr Ranke?"

"I told him that the former occupant had vacated the room, but that I didn't know which room she had moved into. Then the doctor requested permission to use my telephone to call the receptionist. I said all right, and went downstairs into the foyer. But then it occurred to me that the doctor would not lock my room, and I had all my money in the wardrobe. So I went back upstairs and ran into the Signora, who told me to go and fetch her hand-bag. When I'd got back to my room, I found everything in perfect order."

"Was the carpet still where it used to be?"

Lindner was trying hard to remember. He was rubbing his forehead.

"I can't remember. Honestly, I can't."

"I just don't see what makes this carpet so important," said the captain. "Anyway, on the basis of the evidence given, I'm going to order..."

"Pardon me for interrupting," Elder said, "But would the *Signora* and Mr Lindner kindly go over into the adjoining room? I wish to say something."

"All right. On the basis of the evidence you people have given, I am regretfully compelled to detain both of you anyway."

"I was afraid this might happen," Elder remarked sadly.

"Please, sir..." Linder stuttered.

"Be quiet, Enrico!" Signora Relli commanded. "Justice is on our side, and I have confidence in this detective. He is a lot brighter than the captain, and will never let the police make fools of themselves. I've spoken my mind. Do to me as you choose."

Captain Vuyder turned pale as the white of his eyes.

"You people will be disappointed with the chief inspector, I'm afraid. Sedlintz, Ulrik. Escort the *Signora* and Mr Lindner to their respective rooms, will you? They're not allowed to speak to each other. Put a guard to keep watch before each door."

"What about Vangold?" Elder asked. "Is he to be permitted to move without restriction? He has no alibi, and the dagger..."

"Right. Mr Vangold, too, is under strong enough suspicion, and that warrants his being placed under house arrest."

"Then there is also Prince Sergius and Maud Borckman," Elder went on ruthlessly. "Several witnesses saw them in the corridor, and they haven't got alibis either."

The captain was perplexed. At last he tumbled to the fact that once again he had got caught in a trap this man Elder had set for him.

"We will interrogate them," he said grimly. "And if necessary, they will be detained. Any suspect can be detained for twenty-four hours..."

"... provided there is likelihood of their attempting an escape. But not even the tiniest kitten can leave this place unobserved."

"You're wrong, dear colleague. Why, Mrs Villiers, for one, has disappeared without a trace. You may go, Sedlintz."

"Good show, Mr Detective," said Signora Relli as they were leaving."

"Mr Chief Inspector," the captain said sternly. "In the course of your investigation you have gathered several pieces of information, and these you have kept from us and then produced them here with stagy effect. I acknowledge your exceptional capabilities, but the way you've been acting is an offence against the rules of the service."

"You requested me to abstain from taking part in the investigation. I did so nevertheless only to save the force from a painful scandal."

"What sort of scandal?"

"Until now you have detained three persons. On the same basis you ought to detain two more. That makes it five persons. Five influential people, of whom at best only one could be the culprit. This means that four of them are going to raise hell in the papers, and I don't blame them."

"Who are the other two persons?"

"Prince Sergius and Maud Borckman."

"We'll have them up for interrogation. Lieutenant Ferguson will go and get them up here."

Markheit rose.

"I should not, of course, interfere with the business of the police," he said. "However, I would say that Elder has been acting with the best of intention. Why provoke a scandal while we know nothing for certain?"

"So long as we know nothing of Mrs Villiers's whereabouts, we've got to detain every suspected person. It is unfortunate that the Medical Corps cannot give us sufficient guarantee," he added in an oblique remark aimed at Markheit.

"This has to be accepted, I'm afraid," Elder said with a sight. "Although, if you ask me, Mrs Villiers has never left the hotel."

"What makes you say that?"

"Anyone who is about to leave the hotel would hardly attempt to bribe a sentry to get a letter smuggled out. She would want to take it out herself."

"I'll accept that. In which case we'll go through the whole place, all the rooms and other premises, every nook and cranny, this very day."

The prince arrived along with Maud. Sergius was already dressed in his dinner-jacket, ready for lunch. He was quietly pulling on his white gloves.

"Your Excellency, *Signora* Relli and Mr Lindner saw you in the corridor, close to the spot where the murder was committed, immediately after the act had been perpetrated."

"In the corridor… Yes… I was coming to the staircase with Miss Borckman."

"You didn't notice anything suspicious?"

The prince's answer came slowly.

"I heard some noise coming from Room 70, which was occupied by Mr Vangold, but I knew that he was down in the restaurant."

"So?"

"I left Miss Borckman at the staircase for a moment to go back and take a look..." He hesitated.

"And you opened the door," Elder prompted.

"That's right." He relapsed into silence.

"What did you see?"

The prince said very softly:

"I saw a white-haired man stabbed to death."

"This confirms the evidence *Signora* Relli gave," Elder nodded. "Somebody opened the door of the room after she had carried Dr Ranke's body over to Number 70."

The captain tapped a penholder on the table. "I am conducting this interrogation."

"I'm sorry."

"What did you do next?"

The prince's hand was trembling, and so was his voice.

"I told – er – Miss Borckman that she'd better retire to her room... I would withdraw to mine too... So we would not get involved in this affair... Can I get some water to drink, please?"

Lieutenant Ferguson obliged by filling a glass for him.

"Thank you."

"Did you run across anybody in the meantime?"

"Mr Lindner came up the stairs."

"And after that?"

"I waited until Miss Borckman retired into her room, then I withdrew as well."

A pale-faced Maud was watching the frail old man's agonizing embarrassment with dismay.

"Will Your Excellency please go over into the adjoining room," said the captain, and motioned to Sedlintz, who had just returned, to follow the old man.

From the doorstep, the prince shot a concerned glance at Maud.

"You may go. It's all right," she said.

The prince bowed his head and left the room.

"Maud Borckman?"

"Yes."

"You are a person of independent means?"

"No. I am an assistant to Professor Decker."

Markheit got up in amazement.

"What!" he exclaimed.

"What is there to be surprised at?"

"But... Don't you know? The man who is dying of bubonic plague... Why, he is Professor Decker... Hullo!... Bring some water, somebody! Give us some brandy. Quick... Put her on the sofa."

On hearing that piece of news from Markheit, Maud had fallen into a deadly faint.

21.

Bewildered, the captain scratched his head.

"Well, I'm blowed."

"Do you feel better?" Markheit asked Maud.

"Yes... I do."

She sat up on the sofa, and slowly got to her feet.

"How... is... the professor?"

"A case of bubonic plague. Not much hope. He's been unconscious all the time, runs high fever and typical symptoms of sepsis. Swollen lymph nodes... In other words, he is past help. There is nothing we can do. The doctor keeps applying Palmyra ointment to reduce pain and the itching."

"Is there no hope?"

"Well, you know... Bubonic plague is certainly... Poor fellow. I feel sorry for him. He is such a great man."

"Miss Borckman," said the captain. "How do you explain your boss's failure to inform you of his arrival? Did you and the professor part in anger?"

"Oh, no. The professor is very fond of me, and..." The words stuck in her throat.

"Maybe I can help you," said Markheit. "I spoke with the patient for a few moments. He came here incognito. He wanted to catch an erring collaborator without calling in the police." He directed a meaningful look at Maud.

"Do you have any knowledge of this matter?" the captain inquired.

"I don't. It can have absolutely nothing to do with me."

"What do you know about the crime that was committed in Room 70?"

"Quite a lot."

"Please tell us."

Maud's answer was soft and straighforward.

"I killed Dr Ranke," she announced.

22.

A moment of silence followed, then the captain banged the table with such force that it made the objects on it leap and dance.

"Oh, blast!"

"I don't understand this," she said in amazement. "I am going to make full admission of guilt. Dr Ranke sent me a letter at 11 o'clock in the evening, the day before the murder. He'd been here the previous day, seeing a patient. But it was only on the following day that he diagnosed the plague. This is that letter."

She handed it to the captain, who read it. It said:

"*The multiple murderer Borckman and his daughter can hope for mercy from no one but me. Be in the foyer at 3 a.m., and bring the the notes with you. Dr. R.*"

"What are these notes he mentions?"

"I've no idea."

"Who is this 'murderer Borckman'?"

"He is my father."

"Where is he now?"

"I don't know. When his ghastly crimes had been found out, he disappeared from Moscow. My mother and I left Moscow and Russia, and settled in Batavia, and there Prince Sergius, who is widely known to be a philanthropist, extended to us his protection and supported us."

"What was it Dr Ranke wanted from you?"

"He wanted to blackmail me. I turned up for the meeting at the appointed time. He threatened to expose my parentage. He said he'd let everyone known that I am the daughter of a multiple murderer, unless I obtain ten thousand Dutch florins for him from the prince."

"Yes?"

"He gave me until the following day."

"What happened in the corridor next day, when you and the prince were seen together, roughly about the time of the murder?"

"The prince went to his room to get his gloves. He never goes to lunch without them. During that time Dr Ranke emerged from Mr Lindner's room and he demanded money. I followed him, saw the light dagger on the table, and plunged it in his back, and then hurried after the prince. He was astonished to find me waiting outside his door, but he said nothing. Once again we walked past the Seventies rooms, and as we got to the staircase the prince said he was popping back for a minute. When he came back he told me he'd like me to go to my room."

"I am arresting you on the basis of your admission of guilt."

"That is as it should be. I wish you would permit me to attend to Professor Decker. I suppose it makes no difference where I am being kept under arrest."

"I can't give you such permission."

Ferguson entered. He seemed to be agitated.

"Beg to report, sir. The prince has said he wants to make a confession. He says he killed Dr Ranke."

Captain Vuyder had a fleeting impression he was losing his mind.

23.

"Now, that is just not true," Maud declared. "The prince believes that by sacrificing himself he can save me."

As she was saying these words, the prince entered.

"Come off it, Maud," he said quietly. "I killed Dr Ranke. I'd done it before knocking on your door. He was standing in Lindner's room, with the door open. I heard him speak on the phone, asking the hotel operator to put him through to Room 72. I was seized by a fit of rage. I snatched the receiver from his hand, and spoke some rude words to him. He laughed at me. Then he turned to go to your room. There was the dagger, lying within easy reach. I snatched it up, and…"

"This is not true!" Maud cried.

"No use trying to save me, my dear. I did it. Arrest me."

Elder said nothing. He was busy making notes in a notebook. From time to time the captain would look at him. His feelings about the man kept changing.

Eventually, he motioned to Sedlintz, then turned to the two persons he had been interrogating.

"I have noted what you people have said. I should like you to return to your respective rooms and stay there until further orders."

The prince and Maud left the room. Sedlintz went along with them in order to post sentries to guard their rooms. The captain turned to Elder.

"Devil of a business, this. I've never seen anything like this. As many as three offenders for one murder case!"

"Four offenders. The blood-stained table cover was found in Vangold's coat pocket."

The captain was studying his finger nails.

"Umph. I saw you make take some notes," he said softly.

"Yes. I wrote down the principal points of this case."

"Oh, really. And who do you think is the most suspicious?"

"The one who caused the carpet to disappear."

"And why is that?"

"Because he or she was the last person to leave the room. Which means that he or she had hidden himself or herself. That is, he or she had been there when the first suspect arrived, and having watched the body taken away, he or she removed the carpet from the room."

"And this person cannot have been the prince, or Lindner, or Miss Borckman or *Signora* Relli?"

"No, sir. Three people all came across each other following the murder. And none of them had the carpet with them."

"I think the Italian woman is the most suspicious of all."

"They're liable to suspicion, all of them. Each had a few minutes without an alibi at the same time the murder was committed."

Markheit got up.

"I'm off for lunch. Just tell me one thing, Elder. What do you think of this case?"

"It seems to have bogged down. I think we had better let the suspects move about freely in the building, so we can keep them under surveillance."

"But while we have no information about Mrs Villiers's whereabouts, I'm obliged to follow this course of action," the captain said curtly.

"What you might at least do, sir, is to let us mount a search for the carpet."

"How do you propose to proceed?"

"We'll go through all the rooms. It's a carpet of about six feet by ten. It can't have been hidden anywhere except in a wardrobe or under a bed. Find the carpet and you'll have found the murderer."

"All right. You may go through the rooms."

"It'll be an enlightening exercise, quite apart from the carpet," said Elder, and the two of them were off.

24.

The young man woke up. It came to him as no surprise to find that had been sleeping in a bath. Nor was he astonished to find that he was wearing a toupee and nothing else. Occurrences like this had of late become more or less part of the daily routine with him. What did give him something like a pop-eyed look was the spectacle of water running from the tap, overflowing the bath and inundating the bathroom floor.

Where was he?

Slowly, it was beginning to dawn on him... Lee Shing... Bruns... Dr Raleigh and the mimosa flowers...

He turned off the tap. The sound of someone snoring came from the adjacent room. Come on, get out of here, there's going to be trouble in this place, he told himself. He was dismayed to discover that his smock, along with some bits of cold meat, was lying soaked on the bottom of the bath. In the other room, Bruns was sound asleep between the sofa and the table, his head resting on an upturned armchair. The sun was about to come up.

Felix ran to the wardrobe. He had no moral inhibitions. He was on the run. If they catch him, he's going to put a bullet through his head. Aside from everything else, the murder case would be enriched by new evidence.

He strewed pieces of clothing all over the place. He was looking for one that was of the poorest quality. Eventually, he selected some baggy summer clothing.

Now came the most difficult part – the portly fellow was some six inches shorter than him. There was a jacket whose sleeves reached to his elbows, and a pair of trousers that reached just below his knees.

He was rummaging wildly. That fool might wake up, and then it would be all over with him. What was a doctor without clothes doing in his room, he was certain to ask himself.

Felix pulled out all the drawers, one after the other. There was plenty of correspondence lying about. One large drawer of the bureau contained a carpet, six feet by ten, rust-coloured, of course. That wouldn't do. But the sight of the content of the other drawer made him jump like a bean.

That one contained about a score of handguns of various makes and one hand-grenade. What was this? An automatic, an old-type six-shooter bulldog, bands of cartridges... What-ho!

Whaddya say to this meatball? Some sick man. Felix pulled out the next drawer.

This one was stranger still. Lying demurely at the bottom was a machine-gun, smug as a slug in a jug.

A machine-gun! In a room of the Grand Hotel! A carpet and a machine gun. And a solitary gas-mask for good measure.

But nothing was in sight in the way of clothing. This was enough to drive one to despair. What on earth was this arsenal there for? It was inconceivable.

He went back into the bathroom. He opened the window. He heard the sound of voices drifting out of one of the open windows across the way.

"It's not my fault that I'm here, you know. Nobody has the right to force me to work."

"You're wrong, Mr Haecker. You are liable to do work throughout the duration of thequarantine," said another voice, a severe one. It was Wolfgang.

"All right. But then you go and make Governor Shilling work too. I wasn't loitering outside the Grand Hotel because I was desperate for some work to do."

"Oh you weren't, were you? Well, I want you to know that our personnel cannot cope with this swollen occupancy, and I am empowered by the goverment to select auxiliary staff from among persons confined here on Treasury expense."

"I refuse to work," Haecker said.

"He's right, guv," said the old news vendor. "We're detained here under enforced isolation for the purpose of medical observation."

"You'd better shut up!" Wolfgang rapped out menacingly. "Your board here will be changed drastically if you people refuse to work. You'd better keep that in mind."

"In that case, I'll sue you!" Haecker shouted. "We're living here two to a room, anyway, and this is against regulations in the event of a quarantine."

"Suppose I offer to pay you for the work? Eh?"

"I won't take no bribes."

"So. Well, then let me tell you this. If you refuse to work, you're not getting any food."

"I'll get hold of some grub all right. If you think they'll sentence me for larceny, you're mistaken. This is an emergency.

I have Mr News Vendor here for a witness. And Miss Lidia, too – the lady who's also been sentenced to forced labour."

"Now there, you see, is a person whose conduct you'd do well to copy. She earns two or three florins a day from tips."

"What I'm after here is peace and quiet, not tips."

"Fine," said Wolfgang. "Now you go and get that uniform from off the rack, put it on, and report to bedroom-waiter Martin on the next floor. If you don't, your board's going to be just plain soup and bread and nothing else."

"Fine. I'm trying to slim, anyway."

Haecker was paying little attention to what Wolfgang was saying to him. He was reading the papers and magazines in the news vendor's stock.

"As for your having fun, you'll have to do your reading during the day, because I'm going to cut off the electricity in your room."

"You've no right to do that," Haecker protested.

"He is right. You have no right to do that," pronounced the news-vendor-turned-legal-authority.

Wolfgang walked out of the room.

"That brazen-faced, cheeky bastard," Haecker fumed. "Wants to exploit a couple of poor fellows because we've been isolated in this posh place."

"It's Lidia who's spoilt him. That woman appeared to be a reliable and trustworthy alcoholic, and then she goes and hires herself as chambermaid."

The light in the small room went out. Wolfgang had carried out Threat Number One.

"Blast it all!" Haecker swore. "It's only seven o'clock, and I can't go to sleep before ten. That bastard thinks he can put pressure on me this way."

"We're going to have fun all the same," said the old man, and he started grinding his barrel-organ. "This is something you can do even in the dark."

"I wish I could sleep all day like this damned sluggard here," he said, pointing to the corner where the native hawker of fancy goods was snoring. "He won't press this one to work for him."

"That's because he's coloured," said the old man, cranking his instrument. "They don't like coloured folk in these parts, except for bellhops."

For some time the barrel-organ's was the only sound that was heard.

"Listen," Haecker spoke. "That dumpy rotter just across there – he usually goes down to the dining-room about this time. What about me going and helping myself to some drinks and cigarettes in his room, eh? We deserve a good time, too, I say."

"Not a bad idea, that. Should you find some cash over there, better not leave that lying about there, either."

There was now only the sound of the barrel-organ. Haecker crept over and through the window, into the bathroom across.

Splash! What the bloody... He stifled an oath. What was this? The bathroom was swimming in water. He walked about seven steps, then switched on the light.

He stopped in his tracks, thunderstruck. Facing him was a naked man wearing a gas mask and pointing a machine-gun at him. Haecker looked at the man, paralyzed with fear. His tongue and lips refused to work. The MG swung upwards – at last this galvanized him into action. He stretched out one hand, but from the opposite side the gas-masked man's fist shot out, giving him a whopping sock on the jaw that sent Haecker flying backwards into the bath amid tremendous splashing.

All that time the old man had kept on grinding his instrument. Some ten minutes later he heard a slight noise at the window, and vaguely saw a shadow enter through it.

Aha, he thought, Haecker, the plucky jobless chap was returning. He couldn't have been more wrong, for the arrival in the darkened room was that of a gentleman whose attire consisted of a gas-mask and nothing else.

"What've you brought?" the old man asked the shadow that was groping about the clothes rack.

"Hush," it replied.

"There must be some trouble," thought the news vendor as he mechanically continued to grind his barrel-organ. He wasn't unduly concerned, as he was sure he would soon learn the reason for the shadow's silence.

He got the impression that his room-mate was getting undressed. A shoe dropped with a thud.

Five minutes later the door creaked. The fellow had slipped out! Surely he wouldn't have done some dirty work? Where had he gone? He continued turning his barrel-organ, but he was a worried man.

Ten minutes afterwards, a young man reported for work to Martin, the bedroom waiter.

"The boss told me to come here for work," Felix said, for he was the young temporary employee.

"So you're that stevedore fellow, eh?"

"That's me."

"What in the name of God is this clobber you've got on?"

Felix gave himself the once-over. He wore a jacket uniform with golden golden-buttons, which was perfectly in order. However, he had put on a pair of awfully tattered morning coat trousers, which was part of the native fancy goods hawker's raiment. Not quite the sort of thing that was de rigueur for a hewer of wood (and drawer of water) whose duties he was supposed to be discharging. But what could he have done? He had been compelled to get dressed in darkness.

"And these shoes!"

Felix looked down. Good God! He had a momentary fit of dizziness. He was wearing a pair of white tennis shoes, one of which had a brown stain on it.

25.

"Well, you know, fact is, the boss had cut off the electricity, and I was compelled to put my things on in total darkness," he said after regaining his power of speech.

"Oh, all right. Go to recess No. 90, next to the staircase. I'll send you a pair of trousers later. You'll find the bell panel just across. When you see a number light up, go into the guest's room. If an order is placed, ring the restaurant on the house telephone. In case you want to be told something you don't know, I'm on duty on the fifth floor. You can ring me there."

Felix did as he was told. He sat down, made himself comfortable, and lit a cigarette. He had had the presence of mind to stuff the gas mask with cigarettes before climbing through the window. They were golden-tipped and bore the name "Bruns". Aha. Fellow had his own cigarette papers filled with his own special tobacco brand. Rich people do that, by and large.

A number lit up on the panel. Number 60. Felix went to Room 60, where he found a quite good-looking young chap.

"I say, my man, what do you do at this place when you want your things laundered?" the occupant enquired.

"I am new here, sir. But I believe we have a laundry in the house."

"Then get the laundress sent up to me, will you. My name is Erich Kramartz."

"Very good, sir."

Felix rang the restaurant, where the head waiter flatly refused to take the order of Room 60.

"Kitchen can't supply laundresses."

"Then send along a cook. She should do just as well."

"I'll call Reception."

"Please yourself," said the new pageboy, and hung up.

He felt an urge to see Maud. Now that his stay at the hotel appeared to rest on a somewhat more solid foundation, his thoughts went out to her like homing pigeons. There must be some serious trouble here, he thought. The enigma of the tennis shoe was the key to a lot of problems. The man who brought that letter was wearing that shoe, no doubt about that. The shape of that brown stain was quite peculiar. Whose shoe could it be, he wondered. It must belong to the native, because both Haecker and the news vendor had been wearing leather shoes. Consequently, it must have been the Malay who had brought that letter. He must have been sent by someone. And at the autopsy he had perhaps carried instruments or things of that sort. Attendants as well as surgeons are needed for that kind of job. He hadn't thought of this then.

He moved off in the direction of the corner of rooms 70 to 80. He drew back quickly. The native was coming towards him with much caution. He was wearing his usual jacket, but below that he was dressed in a pair of loud red-chequered blue pyjama trousers. Like a reptile, he crept noiselessly up to Maud's door. He bent down, swiftly slipped a letter under it, and hurried off. Half of the letter was sticking out under the door, but was soon withdrawn. Maud took the letter. He made for the door.

At this moment the lights on the floor went out. From somewhere in the darkness came the voice of the police officer on duty.

"Hullo! What's up? Is this a short circuit?"

Felix had a hunch that the sudden blackout was connected with the native messenger. Quickly, he walked to the girl's door, and knocked. The door opened a little, and he was about to enter, when he ran into her outstretched arm. She was holding out an object for him, and whispered:

"Take it, for heaven's sake! Take it away, and be accursed!"

Automatically, Felix took the object. It resembled a copybook. Presently, he heard footsteps coming his way. Doors were slammed at a distance. He heard a noise. Somebody bumped against him, and a strong hand grabbed his arm.

"Who are you?"

"The bellboy... What do you want?"

The shadow was approaching Maud's door. Not knowing what on earth he did it for, Felix gave the shadow a shove in the chest that sent it reeling backwards. He then buzzed off in a haste, as he heard voices drawing near, as well as heavy-booted footfalls. He dived into the servant's lodge, and switched on the light. He found himself holding in his hand a blue copybook, which bore the following inscription:

THE PRODUCTION AND APPLICATION OF BANANA OXIDE,
by Professor Richard Decker.

Meanwhile the lights in the corridor went on again. The police officer hurried along, knocking at each door. Nothing happened. Little by little all the noises subsided as people went to bed. Martin came in to the lodge.

"Anything happen?"

"The lights went out."

"That's all right. But otherwise nothing went wrong?"

"Nothing. One guest placed an order. He will have been served by the restaurant by now."

"Take a nap on the bed if you like, but don't take off your clothes. Set the buzzer on the bell panel. I am turning in, too. Good night."

"Good night."

Martin left. Felix opened the copybook.

The Chemical Formula of the Banana Oxide

That was the title of a chapter. Hm. This small copybook had a key role in the whole business. Wasn't it an odd coincidence. No doubt the native fellow had brought word that somebody would come and knock at the door to be handed this copybook. And in between Felix had happened to come by and knocked at the door. Maud had reached out and handed him the copybook, and hastily called down a curse upon his head. The real guy who came to get the copybook had bumped into him at the door, guessed that something had gone wrong, but as the policeman and the room waiter were coming, the fellow was forced to flee.

The light went out.

What was this again? Someone had quietly entered the lodge, unnoticed by Felix (who was standing with his side turned towards the intruder), and switched the light off. Undaunted by the sudden darkness, Felix pocketed the copybook. He now surmised what it was all about.

"Who is it?" he asked.

The reply came in a whisper:

"Give me that copybook."

"I believe it's only fair to point out that I'm not a nervous chap, Mr…"

"Borckman. Peter Borckman."

Felix was astounded. Borckman… Why, that was Maud's surname!

"Well?" The whisper was menacingly icy. "Give it up!"

"What's all the rush? Why don't we have a word about it?"

"What do you want?"

"Are you in any way related to Maud?"

"I am her father."

A pretty state of affairs this was!

"You don't seem to realize the frightful mess your daughter will find herself in if she hands over her boss's confidential notes to you," the young man said guilefully.

"She'll come to no harm. She'll get away and go to some other place. She won't be extradited on account of industrial espionage. You shouldn't worry on that account. Who the hell are you anyway?"

"I'm a pageboy, but, the overzealous chap I am, I'm solicitous about guests' affairs."

There was a gleam in the darkness.

88

"I have a gun, and it's loaded," said Borckman. "If you don't hand over that copybook, I will shoot you to get it."

Should he hand it over? It was possible that Maud's father was really a disreputable fellow who wanted to ruin her life. His scheme must be thwarted.

"All right. Here you are," he said.

There was no way for the man to see in the darkness in which direction he was to go get the copybook. He took a step, pointing the gun. That instant, Felix kicked over the small table that stood between the two of them, and hurled himself sideways. Borckman staggered backwards and instantly had his feet pulled out from under him, so that he measured his length on the floor. He never pulled the trigger – there was no target to shoot at anyway. He jumped to his feet, and got a sock in the face. He hit out at random, but hit only the air. The door shut close, the key was turned in it. Borckman sat in the darkness, locked up in the lodge. The window of the room gave onto the glass roof of the restaurant. The mystery man knotted a bed sheet and several covers together, then climbed down a floor.

26.

Felix emerged into the corridor. Which way was he to go now? The sudden onrush of light blinded him slightly. He made up his mind that he should go and see the girl. He had barely taken one step when out of the blue, he was blindsided by someone darting forward from a spot where it seemed as if he or she had sprung forth from the floor, and brought a dagger down upon him. Felix could not fend off the thrust, he tumbled sideways a little, and the dagger, which had been aimed at his cervical vertebrae, hit his shoulder and slipped down his chest, slashing his skin open, but failing to make a deep wound. Felix grabbed the wrist of the hand that held the dagger – and stopped in his tracks in amazement.

The man with the dagger was Prince Sergius.

"You…"

The dagger dropped to the floor. The prince looked at him in alarm.

"Yes… I decided to kill you," he said, breathing heavily. "You're not going to wreck Maud's life… I – I'll kill you if you want to take away – er – that copybook."

A portion of the copybook was sticking out from the young man's pocket. He glanced back towards the door, from where he had come.

"First of all, we'd better go away from this spot. I must have a word with you, Prince. But don't be edgy like you were just now. He took the prince by the arm and led him away.

Prince Sergius stopped. He looked at the young fellow with misgivings.

"Where do you want to go?"

"To see Maud."

"No!"

What Felix did next was undoubtedly a manifestation of rather disrespectful behaviour on his part, considering that it was vis-à-vis an elderly aristocrat.. Still, he seized the prince by the neck and frog-marched him along. Having reached Maud's door, Felix knocked, but without waiting for a reply pushed the prince inside, entered the room himself, and turned the key in the door. Maud, fully dressed, was sitting at the table, writing. Now she started up from her seat in alarm.

"Give me some bandage, quick," Felix commanded, "I've been stabbed."

The prince slumped into a chair, and buried his face in his hands. He was panting with exhaustion. Displaying admirable self-restraint, Maud said nothing, but went to the medicine cabinet and took from it some dressing material.

"We've got to be careful," said the young man, "not to let blood drip onto the floor. At this hotel, this sort of thing is apt to lead to complications and embroilment."

He took off his jacket, and opened his shirt.

So far Maud hadn't uttered a single word. Her composure was amazing. She dissolved some sort of tablet in water, disinfected the wound, and bandaged it. After that they carefully obliterated all traces of the accident.

"Switch the light off," Felix said to her. "A duty officer is doing the rounds outside. The light might attract his attention."

She switched the light off, and then spoke:

"Where did you meet the prince?" she asked.

"Out in the corridor, just now. I asked him to come here, but he refused, compelling me to use force."

The air inside the darkened room was heavy with the musty, humid vapours of the sickly monsoon season. Outside, the unceasing rain came pouring down, splashing and gurgling; inside the room, the buzzing sound of a lonely mosquito was heard. The stifling, oppressive smell of lush tropical vegetation had penetrated the room.

"Who are you?" she asked the young man.

What was he to tell her? So far he had posed as missionary, doctor, and bellboy. What else should he become yet?

He lit a Bruns cigarette.

"Careful, Maud," the prince butted in. "He was the one who took the notes."

"What?" Maud sprang to her feet. "You… You are Borckman's man?"

"Now, now. Please let's get this straight. I have got the copybook on me, but I am not Borckman's man. I saw the owner of a rather ragged pair of trousers slip a letter under your door. Thereupon I came here and knocked at your door, meaning to speak with you. Instead, you handed me a copybook, cursed me, and then retired to rest. Meanwhile, in the darkness, a gentleman arrived, and I pushed him away from me. The same person later wanted to shoot me because I refused to hand over the copybook."

"Where is… that man now?"

"I locked him up in Room 90."

Maud went to the door, and listened.

"Stay quiet, you two," she whispered, and swiftly slipped out from the room.

"What a marvellous girl," said the young man. "What grit."

"Oh God," whispered the prince. "And this is all on account of me. I am the cause of all this."

"Would it be impertinent to ask Your Grace about the nature of Your Grace's relationship with Miss Borckman?"

There was silence, save for the unceasing, monotonous hissing of the pouring rain. Two glowing cigarettes were facing each other. The prince's reply came very, very softly.

"She is my daughter," he said.

27.

Maud was soon back.

"He's climbed down from the window. Did you wound him?"

"I didn't. He had a gun. I was glad that I'd escaped with life and limb."

"Give me the copybook."

"Not on your life! You would surely give it up to that repugnant fellow."

"I have to hand it over to him!"

"The hell you do. This copybook belongs to Professor Decker. He may have reported you to the police."

"He hasn't. And he never will. He may already be dead."

"You don't say so."

"Professor Decker is the person who has contracted bubonic plague, which is why we're being kept in quarantine."

The young man gave a whistle.

"That dear, good man," she went on. "I'm sure he came here for my sake, in order to speak with me. He didn't' want to report me to the police. Dr Ranke learned from him that I was in possession of the notes."

"The doctor I murdered?" Felix asked curiously.

"Rubbish. In the meantime I've been put wise it wasn't you who did it. What made you tell me that lie?"

"I could see that you very much wanted that to be the case," he confessed, penitent. "You were under the impression that it was the prince who'd done it. After all, that's why you removed the dagger from the room."

"Er… Yes… But that's neither here nor there. Ranke wanted to use it for blackmail, and was killed for it, in all probability by Borckman. And if he doesn't get the copybook very soon, a lot of people may find themselves in deep water. He's not likely to show mercy at this point."

"Are you from the police? Or are you a private detective?"

"I'm a private detective," he replied without hesitation. "You can trust me – all you have to do is put up with whatever I want to do. Just play along."

"You may be telling me a lie right now."

"I wouldn't put anything past me," he replied sadly. "However, I am sure I'd gladly give up several years of my life to be able to help you."

A long silence ensued. The anxiety and the hot and murky weather weighed oppressively upon them. At last, Maud decided to speak.

"I will tell you everything," she said. "I have to. You have us beaten. The destinies of a number of people as well as ourselves hinge upon your handing over that copybook to Borckman."

The day was breaking. To the dot, as if the sky were clockwork-operated, the rain stopped. It rained from three in the afternoon until four o'clock in the morning, day after day. In between, it was possible to see the steaming of those masses of water as they evaporated in the heat of the day, enveloping the island in an atmosphere of a gigantic wash-house, in reeking clouds ridden with rheumatism, malaria and typhoid.

"You'd better leave the telling to me," Sergius said. "I can't possibly have anyone do this for me. You concede that, don't you, Maud?"

The silence was shattered, but this time, instead of the noise of the pouring rain, by the screeching cry of a parrot that had been startled out of sleep. Beyond the windowpanes the shadows of a few motionless palm treetops were slowly taking shape in the faint glimmer of dawn.

"I am descended from a family of Russian army officers," said Prince Sergius. "My father, General Milenko Sergius, was killed fighting on the side of Admiral Kolchak. I too attempted to flee from the revolution, but never succeeded in crossing the frontier. So I went into hiding in Moscow. After many vicissitudes I bought the necessary papers from a 'document dealer' who sold identification papers made out in other people's names. These papers were made out in the name of one Peter Borckman. That was the first time I'd heard that name. My wife, with our little son and several relatives, taking with her all of my property, had got away during the early days of the revolution and made her way to Paris. Now, armed with the papers made out in the name of Borckman, I could hope to be able to get out and rejoin them. However, things took a different turn. I met Anna Mirskaya and fell in love with her. She was a young student, and a revolutionary. I met her while I was in hiding under the name of Borckman, and of course I never told her my real name. My first marriage hadn't been a happy one. My wife and I thought well of each other, and we both of us loved our little son, but that was all the emotional ties that bound us together. But, after all, that is no excuse for what I did. Bigamy – it's a heinous crime, and odious offence. But passion and a bad marriage are two powerful abettors. I married Anna... We settled in Achinsk, Siberia, far from the noisy politics of the revolution. Two children were born to us – Maud and Peter. For eight years I lived in happiness, working hard to make a living. A diversion I used to indulge in the old days when I had been an aristocrat came in useful to me – I became a hunter. I worked for fur dealers. By then Anna knew my secret, understood it, and had forgiven me. She had long ceased to be a revolutionary – she was a wife and mother. I never longed to get back my former princely life. I was just an ordinary happy man. One day the district police prefect called on me. This man was my best friend, but right then he was cool and aloof to me. He told me that the police were after a man named Peter Borckman, who at the time of the revolution murdered and robbed people. He was a ruthless killer – the prefect placed before me a record of horrible crimes Borckman had committed. He was a monster, Borckman. The prefect told me he gave me until the following day to get away. Can you imagine my situation? My only chance of putting up a defence, in case I'd have been arrested, was to plead that I was Prince Sergius, a former captain of the Cossacks, the son of the hated General Sergius. It would have meant certain death. On the other hand, if I'd be caught as Borckman, they'd string me up on the spot – and with good reason.

"I was forced to flee. I made my way to China. My wife fell ill, she was unable to cross the border, and stayed in Khabarovsk with the children. It was agreed that I should wait for them in Shanghai. But on the very day I arrived in Shanghai I was taken to hospital as I had fallen ill with typhoid. For several weeks I was hovering between life and death. A Russian emigré physician recognized me, and he at once cabled to Paris. By the time I was convalescing, I found by my bedside my first wife, my son as well as my elder brother... They had found me. Escape? It was impossible. I was bound to cause the ruin of two families if it was found out that Prince Sergius was guilty of bigamy. I had no choice but to write to Anna Mirskaya and make a clean breast of things. Then I went to Paris with my family. I had got back into my former milieu of the old days. Anna was an intelligent woman, she grasped the situation. For the sake of our children if for nothing else, there was nothing for her but to accept the turn events had taken."

He had got out of breath and stopped talking for a few seconds. Innumerable raindrops glistened and glittered in the waking sunshine, and long, shiny sword-shaped leaves and dripping coloured hibiscus flowers were swaying in the early morning rush of the warm southerly wind.

The young man lit another of his Bruns cigarettes, and sighed deeply. In every limb he felt the killing weather of the season.

"In Shanghai, Anna met a former colleague of hers, a nice fellow, Professor Decker, a kind-hearted, good man. At the time he was still only a serologist of good repute. Anna and Decker had at one time worked together as interns in Moscow General Hospital. With Decker's help, my second wife travelled to Buitenzorg. The former colleague helped the small family over the initial difficulties before I was in a position to come to their help. Meanwhile, my son, Maud's brother, joined the Dutch colonial army, and is now a captain. Anna died last year. She was a person above the ordinary. Good and kind, intelligent and of great fortitude. Maud has inherited her nature."

The sunshine was getting hotter, and the rain-drenched ground began to send up steaming vapours. A south-westerly wind was bringing from the heart of the island slowly rolling swells of the sulphurous smell of marshland. In the head-splitting wind, palm-leaves would stir from time to time like mollusc tentacles, and huge, purple ferns rustled beyond the window.

"Meantime I was reduced to near-poverty, for that monster – Borckman – had made his appearance. His first letter came to my hand in Paris. He demanded monthly payments of ten thousand francs. It was quite a brief letter, calling upon me to pay the money into an account of a certain number, failing which everyone would be informed that Prince Sergius, using as alias the name of Peter Borckman, was guilty of murders and robberies, and a bigamist. Do you understand this? There was nothing for it – I had to pay up and keep my mouth shut. A terrible retribution had followed in the wake of the crime. I had never seen Borckman, and I had to make payments into African, South American, and Australian bank accounts. During the ten years Borckman was blackmailing me, I was done out of all my money. At last, the terrible blow fell."

The acrid smell of the Bruns cigarettes pervaded the air in the room.

"I will now pick up the thread," said Maud. "Professor Decker employed me as his assistant. In the meantime several serums he had produced had brought him fame. He continued to provide for our upkeep. I worked with him – it was touching, the way he was nice to me. This year he finished his serum, the most important of all – banana oxide. Are you familiar with banana disease'"

Felix's cranium was aching all over.

"Certainly," he answered languidly. "When the unripe fruit is cut off, the shrub becomes diseased and will perish. But bananas need to be transported unripe, otherwise they turn soft, and…"

"What's the matter with you?" Maud asked.

"It's the season… The climate disagrees with me," the young man sighed. "Please go on."

"The drug that preserves the shrub from going bad and perishing after the unripe fruit has been harvested is worth millions. Until now, all attempts to make up a compound like this have failed. Nobody has succeeded in producing anything like it. Decker has. The government has paid him five hundred thousand Dutch florins for it. It was at this point that I received a letter from Borckman. He demanded that I should lay hold of the copybook containing the formula of the banana oxide, and bring it to this place. I was to require to steal something from the noblest person I have ever known, our benefactor! He would consider it to be the final settlement of his claim, he said in his letter. If I refused to play ball, then… What can I say? He knew my father, my brother was an army officer, and there was I… My refusal would spell death to many people. He wrote detailed instructions. I was to get the notes from Decker's drawer when the professor left for Weltewrede to attend a congress there. I was to come here, to Little Lagonda, and put up at the Grand Hotel, taking a room next-door to one that was unoccupied. I would be told when I was to make delivery of the notes. I was forced to obey. When I chanced to get a next-door neighbour, I moved over here, thanks to poor Lindner. When you climbed in through the window I happened to have a meeting with the doctor. He too blackmailed me, as the unsuspecting Decker had told him all on his death-bed. He had followed me here, poor fellow, and meaning to sort out this business himself… That dear, good man – he never reported me to the police. And now… he is dying…"

The putrefying heat had grown unbearable. The garden was steaming, a layer of fumes was spread over it. On the windowsill, a toque lizard, like a miniature crocodile, was gazing into the room, its throat pulsating as it was breathing.

"Chee-chock!" the reptile cried loudly, and waited. "Chee-chock," it cried again, and vanished from the window.

Maud lit a cigarette. No one spoke.

"I think you people are right," Felix finally said. "I'll hand over the copybook." He put down his cigarette, and reached towards his pocket.

There came a knock at the door.

"Who is it?"

"Police."

Noiselessly and quickly, the stranger in the pageboy's uniform disappeared in the wardrobe.

28.

The captain entered, accompanied by Chief Inspector Elder.

"I am sorry," the captain said, "but a lady has disappeared from the hotel. A Mrs Villiers. Did either of you see that lady in the course of the past twenty-four hours?"

"I didn't," Maud said.

Prince Sergius looked deep in thought.

"I did," he said. "She was knocking on the door across from my room, and I even heard someone call out 'yes'. She entered. On the door handle I saw a man's hand in a dark jacket sleeve. I am quite positive about this."

"Can Your Excellency tell me the number of that room?"

"Certainly. It was Number 102."

"Thank you."

The captain went to the telephone.

"You permit me, Miss Borckman?"

She lit a cigarette.

"Certainly. Please go ahead."

He got through to the reception.

"Captain Vuyder speaking. Tell me the name of the person who has taken Room 102… What! Are you sure? Thank you."

He hung up, dumbfounded.

"Well?" Elder inquired. "Who is the occupant of Number 102?"

"Nobody. It has been unoccupied for two weeks."

"Odd, isn't it?"

That was all the comment Elder made. Maud felt a lump in

her throat. That young man was in the wardrobe. And he was not a private detective! He had just said he was, just like he'd made that admission to a murder he had never committed. But who was he? In spite of all the monstrosities, this man had engaged her attention right from their first encounter. Was he a criminal?... No. She felt he could not be one. She hoped he was not one.

"You will become sick, Miss Borckman," Elder remarked.

"Me? Why?"

"You have one cigarette still smoking in the ashtray here, and are already smoking a second one."

He picked up the thick, golden-tipped cigarette Felix had left in the ashtray. The prince was sitting too far away to have been smoking it.

"I didn't like its taste. Someone had offered it to me."

"I can see. It was Mr Bruns. I didn't know you two were acquainted with each other."

She said nothing. She found herself at a dead-end. She had never met Bruns.

"With your permission we will now have a look round in this room," said the captain.

Maud swallowed hard. Her heart was beating like mad. Nevertheless she spoke calmly:

"And... er... What are you looking for?"

"A carpet."

"Am I under detention?"

"By no means. That order has been lifted."

"In that case I'd like to see a written order issued by the prosecutor. So far as I know, no place may be searched without such a warrant."

The captain was taken aback. "Here you are," Elder said, obliging and courteous, producing a warrant from his pocket. "Of course you are not obliged to put up with the slightest irregularity."

It was a proper warrant issued by a court, saying that Chief Inspector Elder was empowered to search any of the rooms at the Grand Hotel without giving any reason for his action.

None were more surprised than Captain Vuyder, but he lost no time in getting down to searching the room. He looked behind the mirror, where it and the corner of two walls bounded a triangular space.

"There's nothing here."

"It can only be under a bed or in a wardrobe," said the chief inspector, and made towards the wardrobe.

Now the young man would be found!

"Nothing here."

Elder opened the wardrobe door. For the space of a couple of seconds he looked Felix in the eyes.

"Nothing in here, either," he declared, and shut the door.

The two men said goodbye and left.

29.

The young man emerged from the wardrobe in agitation, wearing on his head a light chequered coat.

Maud and the prince were still sitting paralyzed with astonishment.

"I'm off. Elder will come back," Felix said, speaking rapidly at a breath. He threw the coat onto a chair.

"Wait!" Maud exclaimed. "We have revealed to you our gravest secrets. You can't have so many crimes on your conscience that they would give you further reason to be afraid of us."

"That is not the point now... If I was guilty of any crime I would own up to it. Unfortunately, I'm only a fool, and ashamed of it. My name is Felix – that's all that's true of what I told you."

"But the police would not be mounting a hunt for someone on account of that. Elder said..."

"That I am the Terror of Java." He made an annoyed gesture. "It was a cunning trick on his part: it was meant to make you frightened of me so you would give me up to him in case you happened to be sheltering me. After all, who would have the courage to give shelter to a robber and murderer? But you are an exception. Elder's trick fell flat. You continued to shelter me, even though you believed him. For that, please accept my compliments and admiration."

"But," interjected the prince, "why didn't the chief inspector arrest you?"

"Because if he had, he would have involved me in the crime wave that is sweeping through this hotel. And Elder knows that I am a square guy. He has no intention of arresting me, just detaining me."

"But why?"

"Because I refuse to get married. But," Felix hastened to add, "this decision of mine isn't final. In due time one comes to realize that it isn't the institution of marriage that's at fault, but..."

There was a rustling sound.

A letter was being shoved in under the door. With a leap like a tiger, Felix was at the door, and he flung it open. There was a muffled thud, a yell – the young man reeled backwards, and pressed both hands over his eyes.

"What's the matter? Maud cried in alarm.

"It seems... I've gone blind... kind of..."

"Show me... Show me, for heaven's sake!"

Felix's eyes were shot with red, and were smarting like mad. However, little by little he was regaining his sight.

"That dirty bastard! He's got a cap pistol or pop gun."

Slowly his vision cleared, but he still felt dizzy. He wasn't sure if it was because of the gas pistol, for he had been feeling unwell for several hours, as if he were suffering from an incipient case of malaria, which was not altogether impossible. Maud dabbed his eyes with a wet cloth.

"That damned rascal!" Felix cried, furious.

The prince had read the letter, and now handed it to Maud.

"At midnight tomorrow the copybook must be on your doorstep. If it is not, by the day after tomorrow, the world will have learned the truth – this time including the fact that Maud Borckman robbed her boss, and that Felix Crickley, the governor's son, murdered Dr Ranke and is guilty of multiple crimes committed at the Grand Hotel. This is the last warning. Borckman."

"What?" Maud asked in astonishment. She now saw the answer to a good many questions.

"Yes. I am Governor Crickley's son – alas. My father lured me home from Paris because... Well, I'm afraid I'd been spending a lot of money there... er... on my studies at the university. You know, in Paris, that's rather an expensive pastime. Why, even a middling butler will take as much as eight hundred francs a month for his services. You know the rest... A promise of marriage... My clothes being locked up. Escaping in a sail-boat, dressed in pyjamas. Coming to anchor in your wardrobe... Could I – Governor Crickley's son – have walked up to the reception desk, dressed in pyjamas, to check in? I'm finished now, for a hundred crimes have been committed in this hotel, and I haven't got a single alibi. What'll I do?"

He had told this tale of woe so pitifully that Maud was moved to laugh.

"Why was Elder looking for you if he didn't seize you?"

"He wants to detain me here till dad arrives. And once he does, I'm done for. My old man's as hard a fellow as ever bit a tiger."

Heavy footsteps were approaching and now halted at the door. In no time Felix was up on the windowsill, leaping off like a grasshopper, soft-landing on the soggy ground. He then broke into a run.

For all the threatening situation and the soldier-like footsteps outside the door, Maud involuntarily gazed after the young man, feeling relieved and happy that he wasn't a criminal.

30.

There came a knock at the door.

Counsellor Markheit entered, accompanied by two medics. He looked grim, and when he spoke, it was in a very frosty tone of voice.

"I am performing my duty in connection with a dying man's wish," he said.

"It's Decker!" Maud exclaimed in alarm.

"Yes. The end is drawing near for him. He has a very weak pulse. It can hardly be felt. Every day I stop for a minute outside the sick-room to hear a report from a dedicated assistant physician who volunteered to attend him. Today he told me he thought Decker wanted to say something but was too weak to do so. He had applied camphor."

"Is he... in much pain?"

"Miss Borckman, do you realize the situation he's in because of you? His body is covered with festering sores, he has egg-size swellings in his armpits, his face is hardly visible, and his skin must be hurting him horribly despite the application of Palmyra oil."

"Stop! Please!" Maud pleaded, gasping for breath.

Sergius drew himself up to his full height.

"There is but one guilty person here. Me."

"In that case, what I've just said goes for you, too. This

kind-hearted scientist has come here to save Miss Borckman from being sent to a penitentiary, and to recover the government's lawful property. Now, even on his death-bed, he begged me, through the assistant physician, not to report what he's said. He asked me to try and recover by fair means the description of the chemical preparation and return it to him. Now I have done this. I am here. You hand over the copybook, I'll take it down to the professor, and I will let you go free. If you don't, I'll report you to the police on Decker's behalf."

Maud and the prince exchanged frightened glances.

"The trouble is, Counsellor... Somebody has taken away the copybook."

"So you refuse to hand it over to me?"

"I haven't got it anymore, believe me. If you would wait just one day..."

"Okay. I'll wait one day. I think Decker would do likewise. But after that, no quarter will be given!"

He nodded curtly, and left.

"What are we going to do now?" asked Sergius.

Maud's reply was resolute.

"We will return to Decker what belongs to him, and face the consequences," she said.

31.

The captain and Elder were standing in Room 102. The ceiling was leaking, a largish patch of it had crumbled, and the opening had been covered with boards.

"Well, I never... Leaving this sort of thing unrepaired in a smart hotel like this," remarked the captain as he contemplated the patchwork.

"Don't forget that the hotel would be totally empty of guests if it weren't for the quarantine," said Elder. "They would have had time enough to look after repairs once the season was over... I say, what's this?"

A half-smoked, golden-tipped cigarette lay on the floor. It bore the name "Bruns".

"This is curious. I think a call on Mr Bruns would be in order. What d'you think?"

"No objection. But what was Mrs Villiers asked to come up here for? And who was the man whose hand Sergius saw?"

"I have formed my hypothesis concerning the case of Mrs Villiers. It is the only solution possible."

"How about letting me in on it?"

"Fine. Let me make it allegorical, though. In short, just because someone is a police captain, doesn't mean he shouldn't know how to play the violin."

"I reject this innuendo. Besides, I only play the violin at home, for my own pleasure. How did you know?"

"Excuse me. That was just by way of an example. I can give you another one. Just because a man comes to the railway station to meet his wife, and a good friend of his also arrives by the same train, it doesn't follow that the man's wife and his friend were travelling in the same compartment."

"But it's highly likely."

"I won't say more because giving out information about the results of an investigation is one thing, and having your suspicions is quite another."

"You mean to say you have a suspect for Dr Ranke's murderer?"

"I do."

"On suspicion?"

"No. I know who the murderer is. I have known from the start."

"Why don't you tell me, then?"

"I have no evidence. Let's go and visit Bruns."

32.

Bruns, his cheeks brimstone-coloured and with deep bluish rings round his eyes, was sitting in an armchair. The face of death – this is the thought that crossed Elder's mind as they entered the room.

"I want t ask you a question, Mr Bruns," the chief inspector said. "When were you in Room 102?"

Bruns sighed.

"Which one is that?"

"One floor up. Its ceiling is in bad repair."

"I've never been in that room."

"But this fag end is from one of your cigarettes."

Bruns took a look at the cigarette.

"And so it is."

"Do you usually offer people your cigarettes?"

"I do. Who doesn't?"

"Mm. You appear to be in low spirits, Mr Bruns."

"You have sharp eyes. I am unwell."

"May I ask what ails you?"

"It's none of your business. Or is that relevant to the case as well?"

"Hey!" the captain rapped out. "I don't like that tone of yours."

"Don't be hard on him, Mr Vuyder. Mr Bruns has every reason to be irritable... Hello! Someone's grinding a barrel-organ. Where ever is that?"

"That too, is a blooming nuisance," the sick man fumed. "This blasted caterwauling has been going on all day long. It's somewhere nearby."

Elder made for the bathroom, as the sound was coming from there.

"That's not where they're making the music," Bruns said quickly. "It's coming from the little courtyard across the way."

Elder pressed the door handle down.

"Hey!" someone said in the bathroom.

"Who is it?" said the captain.

"Name of Haecker," came the reply from within. "What d'you want? I'm havin' a bath."

"You're having company, I see," Elder said to Bruns.

"I am. Not that it's any of your business. He is a docker named Haecker. Got trapped here by the quarantine. An old friend of mine. Comes here to have a bath, and to read illustrated magazines."

"All right, all right. I wish you weren't so angry, Mr Bruns. I'd like to have a word with your friend Haecker."

Bruns walked to the bathroom door and gave it a kick.

"Hey, you! Come out here, and look sharp!"

"Okay, okay, don't get your gander up!"

"Do as you're told. It's the police!"

The captain drew his fingers across his brow. He felt an enervating pressure was getting him down.

It was getting on for four o'clock. The downpour was going to start in an instant. Right before the rain, one would be getting ruffled like the feathers of a bird.

The bathroom opened, and there emerged from behind it Haecker stylishly dressed in gorgeously multicoloured pyjamas.

"What do you wish, gentlemen?" he asked, putting it on, and pulled a "Bruns" cigarette from his pocket.

"What were you doing in Room 102?" Elder snapped.

"Watch your tone of voice!"

"Shut up or I'll give you something you won't forget in a hurry! Put that cigarette down when you're standing before me!"

Elder's words had an astonishingly beneficial effect. Haecker's conduct changed like magic. He stubbed out his cigarette.

"Please, Mr Chief Inspector," he pleaded. "I've changed my ways completely."

"Be quiet!"

"I'll thank you to stop speaking to my visitor in that way," Bruns put his foot in, so to speak.

"You're right. Come on, you, I'll take you downstairs into the wash-house. Just you wait, you rascal. I'll give you what for!"

"Please, sir... Don't take me down there... I – I'll tell you everything. Mr Bruns here'll say okay to you questioning me here, I'm sure."

"Of course. Go right ahead," said Bruns.

"All right. But then you'd better leave us to ourselves, Mr Bruns, as it's just possible that I'll give this gentleman a sound thrashing, and on such occasions Mr Haecker and I prefer to be in private."

"Well, but..."

"You can take your choice, Mr Bruns." Every time he spoke to the American, Elder's voice and the look in his face became most urbane – only to change into its opposite as he turned to face Haecker. "Wait a bit, you miserable hound! I'll give you hell for that! You know me."

Bruns went over to the adjoining room, looking for something. At last he found a suitcase strap, folded it several times, and stepped up to Haecker.

"Elder," said the captain. "You know you aren't allowed to do that while interrogating a person."

"Look here, Mr Vuyder. Hckaer is a customer of my department. Right? Portal Squad is made up of members of the Criminal Investigation Department. We deal with people of a quite different sort from the one you people do in Health. You can't get a word out of this man Haecker unless you..."

"Please, Mr Chief Inspector... I admit... I was there... outside the restaurant... But I never touched the bicycle."

"So you deny it flatly, eh?" said Elder, pretending that that's what he was interested in. "So it wasn't you who took it to pieces?"

"That was only later... It happened afterwards... Slips said he'd get me mixed up in it anyway if I refused to take it to pieces... So I went along and did it. But it wasn't me who sold 'em, except for the lamp and the transmission. But even them I sold for almost a song, sir."

"Listen, Haecker. I'm sick and tired of you. I tell you what you should do. Go over to one of the British colonies. Let the police force there get something hot to handle for once. I've had just about enough of you. If you promise me you'll remove yourself far from Java for good, I'll let you go free."

"An' you're not goin' to hit me?"

"That's quite another matter. It's up for negotiation, though, provided you'll tell me what you were doing in Room 102."

"Really, I didn't..."

The strap stirred.

"Really, I didn't feel bad at all there... When they put me there, into that cubby-hole, where the old man' grinding his barrel-organ, I would often climb over here... when the room was empty... and... I would swipe some cigarettes... But I'd never touch cash! In the evenings I'd slip out of that cubby-hole, and would go to sleep in Number 102 because..."

"Where did you get the key?"

"I've got a master-key."

"Where did you get it?"

"I made it myself. From a wire-mattress... You said you wouldn't hit me!"

"I didn't. Come on, keep talking."

"And that was..."

"Don't tell me lies! How was it when a woman and a man met there?"

"I won't..."

"What!"

"I – I won't deny it. One evening somebody did come in... I had just enough time to go hide in the wardrobe. I didn't see anyone, just heard someone walk up and down. There was a knock at the door. A woman came in."

"What did they talk about?"

"They spoke little. He said... but he was very angry... He said: 'What do you want from me?' He was quite furious, kind of spitting out the words, when she spoke an' said: 'I'm done for... When Arthur finds out about it, he'll do away with you guys... And this time there'll be no getaway,' Then he says: 'Is it money you're after?' Says she: 'No! You've missed the bus, you reptile! You thought you'd just walk out on me like that, didn't you. I've sacrificed my whole life... I detest Villiers...'."

"Go on."

"That's all I know."

"Careful. Give me no more lies or I'll..."

"I heard nothing more, sir."

Elder knew his men. He was aware that Haecker was keeping back something, but he also knew that he would never tell him about it because he – Haecker – would get himself into trouble if he did.

"Why are you blackmailing Bruns?"

"I'm not..."

"Take care!"

"I'm not denying anything, sir. I've just come over secretly to get some food. And there was this naked chap here that knocked me down. When I came to, Bruns was still snoaring. I looked round... and in the drawer... I found some letters... They had been written by a lady..."

"You rascal!" Elder grabbed him by the throat, and shook him. "Cad! You lied to me!"

But Haecker said nothing. Once again Elder realized it was no use. Haecker would keep mum. For if he talked he would be guilty of betrayal. He would rather face being beaten within an inch of his life.

"Now, listen, you blackguard! You will report to my office each morning and evening. The day you will fail to show up, I'll have you arrested. Have you got it?"

"Yes, sir."

"We can go now, Mr Vuyder."

Now that the coast was clear again, Bruns re-emerged from the adjoining room.

"Tell me, you leech. Is there a way for me to get rid of you?" he said angrily. He sighed, and lit up.

"There is no way," replied Haecker. "From now on, I want to live a nice and cozy life. You're a gun-runner. A guy like you makes heaps of money, and can well afford keeping a well-meaning blackmailer. What can you offer me in the way of food?"

The listless man with the butcher's appearance sighed sadly.

"Go ahead and have whatever you want brought here," he said. "Damn crook," he added for good measure.

Haecker didn't take the insult to heart very much.

"Tell me, Mr Bruns," he asked, "what's the matter with you? You keep sighing all the time."

"It's none of your business, understand? Go eat something and get some sleep, and leave me alone. You won't be sponging on me for long anyway. I'll live on a few more weeks at most."

"That's a lot more than one day. Guess it'd be too much to hope for a steady job. Still, why shouldn't you go on living longer'n that?"

"Because I'm dying."

Haecker lit a cigarette.

"Why, man, if you didn't have this run-down look and your mug wasn't this yellow, one would say you're tough as nails."

"I used to be... Not so long ago. I used to trade with pirates and robbers. You got to have guts for that kind of job. Now dry up and leave me alone. I wonder why I'm putting up with your blackmail, when I've been cursed, and my number's up."

"But if it isn't, the letter I've pinched from your desk drawer will land you in jail for ten years."

For a while after this, silence reigned.

"This *is* a horrid season here," Haecker mumbled. "I'm getting old. Years ago I wouldn't care a damn what season it was." And with a painful look in his face, he swallowed.

"Now leave me alone and stuff yourself if you want to," the stout man said in a harsh, whimpering voice. But Haecker once again drew his hand across his sweating forehead.

"I can't. My appetite's gone."

"What do you feel?" Bruns enquired.

"I feel a pressure on the top of my head."

"I have the same feeling. And my feet are cold, and my hands are damp. At times I see lots of tiny dots flicker before my eyes, just for a few moments."

Haecker turned pale.

"Is it possible... that a curse is infectious?"

"I don't think so."

"I too feel...as if I'd been cursed."

"It's quite possible," Bruns replied. "If my curse on you works."

33.

Felix realized that he could not stay in the garden for long. Pressed close against the wall, he was walking on soft and soggy ground, made soppy by the rain. Eventually, he came to a window. This was no room, he thought.

He glanced about, then hoisted himself up, and presently was inside. He had been wrong: it *was* a room, though a plain one. Walls painted instead of being hung with paper; a tin washbasin, an old-fashioned bed, and a mirror in a seedy frame.

No doubt one of the housemaids lived in this room. Ho! There was a string of coral beads hanging on the side of the mirror. This was the room that woman with the dreadful voice had spoken of when she was shouting up to him, in the belief that he was this fellow Martin. He lay down for a little on a worn leather sofa that had been brought here instead of to the junk room. It was odd how tired he was. It wasn't malaria, he hoped. He had nausea, and felt his hands and feet grow numb. He had had this feeling several times during the day, but each time it had lasted for just a short while.

It stopped again as soon as he had lain down.

Upsy-daisy!

He spotted a key on the table. It was a master key. That was the one that female had been yelling to Martin to bring it down to her. This will open the locks of all the doors! Hurrah!

He would lose no time in moving into an unoccupied room. What was more, he would have a bath! He was longing for an opportunity to shave, for his chin was bristling shockingly. And now he had a master key! Oh God... A razor wasn't such a valuable item – he would send ten razors to the man... In short, with the help of this master key he would be able to lay hold on a razor as well.

Ugh!

He shuddered at the thought. The things the pressure of necessity forces a man to do! He pocketed the key, and set off on his hunt for a razor. He hid in a dimly lit corner of the corridor. Way down, a door was just opened, and a man in a grey suit emerged from it. He turned the key in the lock, put it into his pocket, and started going down the stairs. The fellow was going down to the foyer or to the restaurant. Here goes!

He opened the door. The master key turned smoothly in the lock. He entered the room.

He didn't have to rummage about for long: the whole shaving-kit – razor, shaving-cream, shaving-block and razor-strap – lay on the glass shelf above the washbasin.

Quickly, he slipped the razor and the cream into his pocket. They were first-class. The razor had a beautiful blade, with a mother-of-pearl handle. Written in gold lettering on the handle was this name, "Sydney Crick". He took nothing else, save a bar of soap and a towel, and then hurried off.

Now then. Which room was unoccupied? The mezzanine was full up – that much was certain. Therefore he stole up the winding-stairs to the second floor.

Well, well!

A servant was standing by the food lift. Felix sat down, pressing close against the wall.

"Hey, you!" the servant shouted down the shaft of the food lift into the restaurant below. "Get a move on!"

"Stop yelling!" Director Wolfgang had turned up in the corridor.

"Sorry, sir. But the marquis is impatient."

"You mustn't shout, even then. What about the carpet?"

"There was a little mix-up, sir. I had laid it out into the corridor before I would take it to the store-room. And... Well, it just disappeared."

"What kind of a cock-and-bull story is this?"

"Martin said he'd taken it in error to Mr Bruns's room. But I didn't see it there."

"He'll be fired for this. He'll be taken to the police station," Wolfgang bawled. "Where's the carpet gone from Bruns's room?" The hotelier was beside himself.

"Maybe it's been stowed in a drawer, sir. That American dislikes carpets and may have shoved it in some place."

"Why didn't you people go and have a look?"

"Because... We mustn't do his room except when his present. And none of us dares touch his drawers. He's a rough customer, that gentleman."

"Well this will be fixed yet. This is outrageous! If you don't get that carpet back by tomorrow, you've had it. Understand?"

"Yes, sir."

The small lift was humming: the marquis's dinner was coming up. The servant took it out, and sent the lift back down.

"That drenched bed linen is still there in Number 102. Get it down tomorrow. And remove the debris of crumbled pieces of wall, too."

The director went away, infuriated. The servant carried the dinner to the marquis. Felix emerged from his hiding place behind the winding-stairs. He had found a room: Number 102 must be unoccupied with its wall caved in. At that moment came a brief humming, and the lift stopped there, having brought up the second course: a nicely roasted half-chicken lay on the platter. He swooped down on it and stuffed it into his pocket, then was off for Number 102.

34.

The mouldy smell of wet plaster filled the room that was vacant because of its broken wall. Felix quickly went into the bathroom and turned on the tap: a thick stream of hot water ran into the bath tub. Even the marvellous prospect that he was going to have a bath failed to dispel the bitter taste in his mouth and his malaise.

Something was not all right with him. He hadn't liked the taste of the roast chicken either, though it was a long time since he'd had a bite. Half of the chicken he had thrown out the window. He fished out all the things from his pocket and placed them on a chair: the master key, the bar of soap and the razor with the mother-of-pearl handle with the name "Sydney Crick" inscribed in it. He then proceeded to take a bath, then, sitting up in the tub, smeared some shaving-cream over his chin and cheeks. He got out of the bath, stood in front of the mirror, and started shaving.

He had just finished shaving one of his cheeks when there came a grating sound from the door lock as the key was being turned in it. They were coming!

Slowly and calmly, Felix backed towards the window, clutching the soap and the cream. He snatched up the master key from the chair. His clothes were too far, on a rack close by the door.

"There. Put the carpet here, there's none in this room anyway," said Wolfgang. "And not a word about this to anyone. We'll have it cleaned next year."

"What on earth may have left this ugly stain on the carpet?"

"A bottle of brandy spilt over it. They should be ashamed. You ought to have asked Bruns – that's all. He said straight away he had thrust the carpet into the bureau."

Felix felt relieved: they were not going to come into the bathroom.

"On second thoughts I think we'd better put the carpet in the bathroom before the bath."

Whew!

He had just enough time to step out through the little window with lightening speed. He was standing there, in the light wall, two floors above ground, hovering between sky and earth, clinging to an iron ladder, stark naked.

"Now that's the limit!" Wolfgang roared. "The cheeky bastard! One son of a bitch comes here regularly to change his clothes... And to have a bath!... Take this stuff to my office. Whichever of these rascals can't account for his change of clothing – I will make him pay for this! Dirty pigs! Peasants! Now get going!"

Felix's garb was taken away. Here he was, grabbing a razor and a master key, with one cheek shaven, the other stubbly, stripped clean of clothing.

He put the key, the razor and the soap into a towel, made the lot into a bundle and tied it onto an arm. The he stepped out onto the iron stairs.

There began a suspenseful hunt for some wearing apparel.

The night was pitch-dark and it was raining in torrents: he was like a drowned rat, with not a stitch on, dry or wet. He could only see three dark windows. The first, to the right of him, was that of another bathroom. He climbed in.

It was a wrong place: light filtered through the chink of that door that opened into an apartment. He could hear a conversation beyond.

It was the widow! There was no mistaking Signora Relli's deep-sounding voice.

"I've had little joy and happiness in life," she was saying. "But there were times when I was happy, which is why it doesn't hurt to reflect that I'm getting old."

"The question is, have you had charity?" said a rasping male voice.

"I believe I have. Why, even the fact that I now have something on my conscience is due to charity. I meant to seek advice from a colleague of yours, but oddly enough, after two brief encounters I've never seen him again."

"I haven't been aware that yet another missionary is living in this hotel."

"What's more, he is a member of the same order you belong to. The same buttons, velvet collar like this, with a great spot in it."

"How very strange. That grey spot is where the velvet became moth-eaten."

"Isn't that remarkable?"

"Hmph. I think I'd better check up on this peculiar fellow-missionary... Now tell me about what it is that weighs on your mind."

"It is a very sad business, and I am seeking advice rather than exoneration because I misled even the police. I told them I'd never met Arthur Bocklin. However, the truth is, he and I used to be together a lot in Singapore."

"Why did you deny that fact?"

"Because... I knew they were asking their questions on account of his wife. And she is here, in the Grand Hotel, under an alias... Her husband believes she is my guest... I'm rather upset about this, but then I'm a romantic soul... You see, she is in love with a young man... She asked me, back in Singapore, to cover up for her before her husband, and that I should write her from here a letter inviting her to come and stay with me for a few days. With my letter, she would be able to leave without difficulty... I did write that letter."

"You acted improperly."

"You see, I am Italian... And here was love, romance, and an unhappy wife... I have since repented that I did, for there was here another woman who loved the boy... They had been lovers for a long time... and she had made great sacrifices for his sake. She too had been a dancer, they used to dance together, but later she married an old and ugly newspaper editor-in-chief just so she might be able to get hold of plenty of money which she would give to Doddy. I am speaking of Mrs Villiers, who has disappeared... Previous to that, she had come and seen me. She cried and fainted. Back in Singapore, the boy had walked out on

113

her for the sake of this woman, and she now had nothing and been left with this old and this disgusting husband of hers and... She said she was going to write to the husband of this other woman, because she wouldn't let go of Doddy."

"What execrable, wretched lives!"

"*Si, si...* Now I realize that. But back in Singapore I still thought it was romance. And Mrs Villiers apparently has found a way of escaping from here. I didn't tell the police what I knew. For that sinful woman lives here under an alias: she checked in as a Mrs Hould. She plans to elope with the young fellow, and she has a lovely small child... That's what I wanted to tell you about, and ask you to help me. What shall I do?"

In the dark bathroom, Felix stood still, listening: he was able to hear every word that passed between Signora Relli and the missionary.

The unclad young man who, with a bundle hanging from his wrist, had been eavesdropping, was not interested in the advice the missionary was giving to the Italian woman, He stopped out onto the iron ladder to resume his indomitable hunt for clothing. He came to the window of another darkened bathroom. He entered. He was sneaking silently. He stopped to listen; then opened the door into the room – and stopped in his tracks on the cold stone floor, filled with dismay.

The small saloon communicated with another room, which was only separated from it by a curtain. Somebody had just set a gramophone going

> *Miss Otis regrets*
> *she cannot come*
> *to lunch today...*

"Come on, stop that loathsome music," said a blonde and buxom woman in an evening gown.

Hilliers, the condensed milk manufacturer, and his wife were the occupants of this suite. A couple from the American upper crust.

"Better stop ordering me what I am to do, Mae," he said, and continued humming the tune, while untying his tie.

"Shame on you! Imagine what the personnel may think of me! Flirting with the chambermaid! An American billionaire!"

Hilliers whistled the tune, took off his jacket and placed it on the back of a chair. She whipped off a diamond diadem that was worth tens of thousands of dollars, and hurled it against the gramophone.

"Answer me!" she screamed in a savage, vulgar manner. "I won't have you treat me like I was your dog!"

There was a look of indifference in his face as he lit himself a cigarette.

"Will you please stop shouting," he replied in a bored tone of voice. "Remember that you're not in a self-service eating joint."

"You atrocious figure! If you didn't like me being a waitress who lists orders of wine and food, why didn't you go and marry some high-class lady? But where's the woman who'd marry a barker? A guy with his damned cheeks covered with powder who stands outside low dives loudly addressing passersby inviting them to visit the place. Why, you still are just the same lowdown guy you were in the old days – a hawker and a barker. For all your millions, you're just the same wretched bastard!"

Humming the tune, Hilliers wound up his watch. The gramophone kept churning out

> *Miss Otis regrets*
> *she cannot come*
> *to lunch today...*

She smashed a vase on the floor. Her heavily made-up chubby face, that had retained little of its faded beauty, was distorted with fury.

"Goddamn con man! Barker! Three-time crook!" she screamed, inarticulate with anger.

"Don't kick up such a racket," he said softly, "or I'll..."

"Give me a thrashing, won't you. Yeah, that wouldn't be past you I'm sure. Faugh!... You chambermaids' johnny."

"Listen, Mae. Stop this, I'm telling you. A chambermaid is just as much a human being as is a chauffeur... My own goddam chauffeur. Don't go thinking I'm a fool!"

"You disgraceful slanderer! Jail-bird!" She too began to undress, going about it in a radical, temperamental way – with one sweeping, forceful gesture, she ripped the wonderful Parisian silk gown all the way down to her waist.

Felix took to flight.

Once again he was standing in the downpour. Trailing him

from very far, filtering through the curtain of the torrential rain, was the muffled sound,

> *Miss Otis regrets*
> *she cannot come*
> *to lunch today...*

35.

Once again he found himself in a bathroom. From there he proceeded with much caution to a dark bedroom. Then...

Someone was coming from the adjoining room. He had just time enough to conceal himself between the wall and the wardrobe. The door opened – in the light that was streaming in, he saw the figure of a chambermaid wearing a pretty head-dress. Three women were sitting beyond the door; they were: the young and lovely Baroness Olga Petrovna, a well-known tennis champion, Ursula Huggersheim, widow of the Knight Von der Frühwart, a lady of at least 70; and Helga Jörins, a Swedish metaphysical thinker, author of a number of scholarly books and founder of the Indian Soul Movement. She was a white-haired woman, tall and gaunt, with a wrinkled face, and wore a pince-nez and a black blouse with a high collar. Helga Jörins (the founder of the Indian Soul Movement) said to the chambermaid:

"I want the bath filled with water of a temperature of 40 degrees centigrade."

Felix was a captive, for the chambermaid entered the bathroom. The water came gushing from the tap.

The two visitors were taking leave.

"I will tell the boy to bring down a short quilt filled with eiderdown for you," said Ursula Huggersheim (widow of the knight Von der Frühwart). "During this wet season, rheumatism attacks you through your legs."

"It is very, very kind of you," Helga Jörins the theosophist, thanked her effusively. "Thank you very much indeed. Please accept as a toke of my gratitude my book on *Female Chastity and Immortality*."

"Thank you. Are you coming Baroness Petrovna?"

"I think I'll just stay for one more minute. Miss Jörins was kind enough to permit me to select a few books... It is just awful to have to go without tennis and sailing during this horrid season. I hope to get some compensation from a few good books."

Baroness Petrovna was a beautiful blonde, with a delicately shaped face and a fine figure, whose attractive shape had been enhanced by her sporting activity. Dressed in a grey and plain tailored costume, she resembled the heroines of Ibsen's plays. Walking with a rhythmical, leisured gait, she ambled up to the bookshelf, and, with her hands behind her, and swinging her handbag on her fingers, studied the volumes.

Ursula Huggersheim (widow of the knight Von der Frühwart) was leaving: she was seen out by the dehydrated elderly beanpole of a theosophist (founder of the Indian Soul Movement).

Felix stood motionless – and his motionlessness became quite concrete-like when he saw what was happening in the adjoining room.

Baroness Petrovna shot a quick glance around, then pulled out one of the drawers of the chest, took out two small-size items from it and slipped them into her handbag. The she found a wad of bank notes hidden beneath some pieces of clothing, took a cut of them and buried it too in her handbag. This done, she pushed the drawer back, and quickly produced her compact to sprinkle her face with a bit of powder, an activity that offers for women an outlet for some of their nervousness.

A thief in the house!

Miss Jörins came back.

"Well, have you taken your choice, my dear?"

"Oh yes. This one, and this here," Petrovna said, taking two books from the shelf at random. "Well, good night."

"They are truly fine works," said the white-haired theosophist, and took a look at one of the books Petrovna had chosen. "This is not bad! Where did you learn to read Old Arabic?"

"Oh... I started years ago... Well, good night."

"Good night, my dear."

The baroness left.

"Your bath is ready, Ma'am," announced the chambermaid, and bowed out.

Miss Jörins went into the bathroom, leaving the saloon deserted.

Felix looked round wildly. His eyes scoured through the room in search of something that was fit to be donned so he would be able to attempt a break out into the corridor... The bed cover!... The white-haired metaphysical thinker was bound to come back shortly.

Good heavens!

He pulled the cover off violently and in the same instant jumped onto the bed in order to climb in between the sheets. Somebody was coming!

He was not quick enough.

It was dreadful!

Buttons was bringing the short quilt filled with eiderdown – but the spectacle that unfolded before his eyes in the light of the adjoining room made him stop dead, aghast.

He saw a naked young man kneeling on the bed.

Buttons, a man with dignified-looking side-whiskers, threw the quilt down, and beat a hasty retreat. As he was hurrying down the corridor, he murmured: "Terrible... It's incredible... Fantastic... Well, I'm blowed – and words to that effect.

He hiccuped several times, and one of his shoulders jerked nervously from time to time in a spasmodic movement as of one suffering from the effect of shell-shock. Several weeks afterwards, the memory of that spectacle would still make him shudder.

Miss Jörins was never after this able to understand the strange behaviour of Ursula Huggersheim (widow of the late Knight Von der Frühwart) in eschewing all association with her, to the point of even dropping nodding acquaintance. After that night, Ursula Huggersheim would give the venerable theosophist the go-by whenever they met.

36.

It was around 11 p.m., and Maud was still reading a book, when there was a knock at her door.

"Come in."

There entered a lady of scary appearance. She was rather curiously attired: coffee-coloured blouse, dark taffeta petticoat, and patent-leather shoes; and one cheek, separated from the other with mathematical accuracy, were covered with a thick growth of hair.

"Shush," said the apparition. "I've got to change. I've brought some clothes." He slightly lifted a bundle from which protruded a sword.

Maud pressed her hand against her mouth to suppress her laughter.

"Just like you!" said Felix bitterly. "Laughing at me in such a dramatic situation."

"Where are you coming from?"

"I wonder myself."

He disappeared in the bathroom, and presently re-emerged, tricked out in Commander Dickman's uniform. The trousers came down to his ankles, the jacket to his wrists, and at the very first movement of his arm an epaulette flew off.

"I must get a shave now," he declared grimly, for he had carefully kept the razor with the mother-of-pearl handle and the inscribed name "Sydney Crick" as well as the soap and the master key.

"You are an awful sight, sporting a half-beard."

"I was fully aware, when I came here, that it would be better to die than face you like this. I'm dying to make a hit with you, and then, when we meet again, you see me looking like a billy goat that's been half-skinned, as in a fairy tale."

With these words, he simply drew the girl to him.

"Maud… Would it alleviate your sadness if I told you that I know everything about you – and still I love you?"

She stood before him sadly, but offering no resistance, and inclined her head.

"What you're saying makes me feel good… And, perhaps, if another time… Ah well – It's all the same now, anyway."

"Listen to me, Maud… In America you and the prince would be able to disappear, and if you two disappeared, I would follow you."

"Too late now. Whatever happens, it's all over with me. Whether it's Decker who will report me to the police, or Borckman making his exposure, I am done for… The most I can hope for is that a few people may be saved at the price of my honour. Give me that copybook, please."

"The… copybook?"

His alarmed look filled her with much anxiety.

"I… I left it… in Number 102," he stammered. "In my bellboy's uniform… It was in its pocket… And they took it away."

37.

"Can't you go back and fetch it?" she whispered.

"The took the uniform to the director's office. The copybook was in its pocket."

She shrugged, and her shoulders sagged dejectedly.

"Then it's all up with me... At midnight, Borckman will come to get the copybook. If he doesn't find it on the doorstep, he will take his revenge tomorrow. And everyone... My father... My brother..."

Desperately, Felix was trying to insist on his brainwave.

"There's only one thing we can do. We will place on the doorstep a letter, instead of the copybook. You will write to Borckman that the notes are in the pocket of a jacket that was taken from Room 102. And I am now going downstairs to the office..."

"No! You mustn't continue risking your honour on my account. A murder was committed in this hotel! And you have no alibi!"

"Look, Maud. Until now, I have been an idler. My life has been rather shallow. But now, everything has changed in the space of a few days. And most of the reason of the change I've undergone is you. My honour matters nothing if yours is in jeopardy. You and I will stick to each other, no matter what will happen."

"Oh. You are being serious?"

He pressed her to him.

"Now you aren't alone in this fight anymore, Maud. I want you to take this seriously, the way I feel about it. Do write a few lines to that man and place it on the doorstep... I'm off."

He swiftly slipped out through the door.

38.

It was evening... Getting on for midnight, the time Borckman was due to show up.

Maud wrote a letter, in which she gave a truthful account of all that had happened. Having finished it, she placed the letter on her doorstep. She then switched off the light, lit a cigarette, and waited.

The rain had stopped, and from time to time plops of heavy raindrops would pierce the silence; the croaking of frogs was heard in the hot night, which was heavy with the smell of rotting vegetation. The island was shrouded in dense mist.

The deep, hollow sound of a ship's horn, drawn out, came from afar; at this time the sea would be shrouded in a thick blanket of fog. Half an hour passed. The heavy raindrops falling with deadly monotony marked the passage of time.

She felt uneasy and distressed. She wasn't afraid of the nocturnal meeting: she was troubled by qualms about Felix. Her cheerful friend with the ardent look in his eyes was liable to get into trouble on account of her.

She heard the shuffling of feet on one of the upper floors. A door was slammed shut. Somewhere water was streaming loudly from a tap. After a time, silence fell. Out in the garden, something dropped from a tree with a thud. The ground was exuding flower scent that was somehow carrying in it the smell of cellars: as it became relieved of atmospheric depression, it was slowly invading the room. She could hear the buzzing of four or five mosquitoes around her, and in a nearby room a clock struck twelve.

It was midnight! Borckman's hour.

The mosquito net creaked: a bat had banged against it. She turned about, wonderfully calm. Emerging from the darkness beyond the window, the motionless top of a palm-tree came into sight, lit by the vague, white-as-a-cloud-of-smoke moonlight.

"Wooee-hee, wooee-hee..." An audacious small mongoose snorted, a rattle in its throat as it clashed with a cobra.

Then there was silence.

One of the two was finished. Was it the mongoose or was it the cobra? Or both?

A mix of air current smelling like mildly rotten-egg that rose from the putrid mangrove marsh, and the smell of the sodden, heavily breathing garden, was wafted along by the post-midnight breeze that was blowing in the opposite direction.

Profound silence reigned, rigid and stiff as raindrops were falling plop-plop. The moonshine grew dim and vanished: dark night invaded the room and stood in the room, an intangible thick black wall.

Maud reached for her lighter, and put a cigarette between her lips.

"No lighting up!"

The voice spoke in the room, but it did not come from the

direction of the door. Evidently, the person who spoke had been staying in the room when she had entered. He had been lying low in here for hours.

Obediently, she put down lighter and cigarette.

"Is that you, Borckman?"

"Yes."

"Then you will have heard what I and that gentleman were talking about some time ago. The copybook is in the office, in the pocket of a bellhop's uniform. I have placed on the doorstep a letter I've written to you – I was not aware that you were hiding in my room. You must give me some more time so that I may be able to get the notes back."

"Need to think this over. Tomorrow there'll be another message at the door. Be quiet!"

She did not see the speaker: his voice came from the farthest corner of the room. She never even turned that way. Suddenly, in the slit under the door the light of the lamp in the corridor went out. In four enormous leaps, the visitor reached the door, pressed the door handle down, and was gone.

For a couple of seconds gloomy silence appeared to have returned; then, on a sudden all hell broke loose.

"I've got you!" thundered a voice, and it was followed immediately by a clattering and thumping and a thud, the noise of running feet, of someone tumbling to the floor, and a cry of distress trailing away:

"Catch him! He's the murderer! Trip him up!"

Bang! Bang! Bang! Three shots rang out.

Maud sat there, benumbed.

The lights went on. Doors were slammed. The corridor filled with noisy disorder, loud voices.

"Are you hurt, Elder?"

"Someone struck me over the head quite hard. Unfortunately, the torch had slipped from my head before I had time to flick the switch. Just bandage my head, will you."

"I fired at random in the darkness. I've no idea if I got him," said the captain. Presently, a babble of voices drowned out everything.

Hotel guests who had been awakened came hurriedly from every direction.

"For God's sake," boomed Wolfgang's voice. "What happened?"

"Everybody please retire to their rooms immediately," said the captain resolutely. "The police will keep order, whatever happens."

At this, it goes without saying, hysterical terror took possession of all those present.

Lonely ladies decided to spend the night together, leaving the lights on until morning. The Marquis de Raverdan, fully dressed and leaning on his walking stick, came hobbling into view, his quivering right hand clutching an antiquated duelling pistol.

Prince Sergius got no farther than the turning. When he saw the assemblage of people outside Maud's door, he fainted. Shilling, the governor of Tonga Island, threw his arm around him in time.

"Somebody fetch a doctor! A man has fainted!" he shouted.

Several women began to scream. The French attaché's five-year-old son howled at the top of his voice. And a deathly pale Director Wolfgang stood transfixed, with drops of perspiration falling from under hair that fell over his forehead.

With much difficulty, order was eventually restored.

Markheit gave the prince a shot in the arm, then proceeded to apply treatment to Elder, who was pressing to his head a piece of blood-soaked rag.

"Maud...," said the prince softly.

"She's all right," Elder said. "We have talked with her. Your Excellency should return to your room. The police must not be disturbed in the performance of their duties."

Once the prince had been led away, they started for Maud's room. Markheit was one of the company. They could not be aware of what had happened there: It was only to reassure the prince that Elder had said that he had spoken with her.

As he reached the corridor telephone, Elder stopped.

"Just a moment," he said, and dialled a number.

"Well?" he said, and listened. "Good job. Thank you, Sedlintz. This is a damn good show," he said, and hung up.

"What was it Sedlintz reported?" the captain enquired.

"I had told him that, should the lights go out once again, he was to race right away to the switchboard, no matter what would happen, and take a fingerprint from the handle."

"Good show!" Markheit said with unintentional appreciation.

"An excellent idea," the captain admitted wryly.

"It is probably the murderer's accomplice who pulls down the handle in order to plunge the place into darkness."

"It is the murderer, if you ask me."

"What makes you think that?"

"I know who the murderer is. He prefers to keep in the shade."

"I know your theory, therefore I don't insist on being told the person's name. But how did you know that a crook was going to call on the young lady at midnight tonight?"

"I'd rather not disclose that either. I have strong reasons to withhold that piece of information. You acted very swiftly and energetically, Captain Vuyder."

"Unfortunately, I probably missed my target in the darkness. That person who hit you over the head – where did he come out from?"

"From a nearby room. I heard a door creak, and there and then I was hit with an iron bar or rubber truncheon."

They had reached Maud's door. Elder knocked.

"Yes!" a calm voice called out.

She looked at her visitors cheerfully. This time she was not putting on a show: her fears and anxieties dispelled, she was ready to meet her fate.

Elder spoke.

"Miss Borckman," he said, "I think the best thing for you to do would be to tell us straight on about all that happened here tonight – insofar as it touches upon the investigation that is in course," he hastened to add.

"With pleasure."

She told them how somebody had written her a letter asking for a meeting at midnight; she told them about the surprise appearance of her strange visitor, and gave a word-for-word account of the conversation they'd had.

Elder reflected.

"In a statement that was taken from you recently, you declared you had no knowledge of any 'notes'."

"I wasn't telling the truth. I stole Professor Decker's description of the banana oxide. I was acting under blackmail from a criminal – I won't tell you anything about what he threatened to expose. I wanted to hand him the notes, but unfortunately I am no longer in possession of them."

"In this case we shall be compelled to take you into custody, Miss Borckman," said Elder, and sighed.

"Of course," she replied calmly.

"Let us go back to your visitor. Are you sure you quoted that person's words correctly?"

"I have a very retentive memory."

"His first words were 'Don't light up!'?"

"Not exactly. He said, categorically: 'No lighting up!'"

"And lastly he said: 'I'll think this over... You will find a message at the door'?"

"Not exactly so. He said: 'Need to think this over'... 'There'll be a message at the door'."

"Thank you. This evidence will make it easy for us to detain one accomplice. Good night, Miss Borckman. I'll get you off the hook if there's a chance, and you'll come to no harm. You can be sure of that. From this moment on, please stay in your room. A sentry will be posted at your door."

In the corridor, the captain asked Elder nervously:

"Why did you tell her we've got one accomplice?"

"Because it won't be difficult to find amongst the natives at the hotel the one who was in her room tonight."

"You spring upon us a fresh surprise," Markheit said. "Now where d'you get this from?"

"It's a typical native custom of using mostly either the infinitive or the verbal nouns instead of the various verbal forms, since conjugation of verbs is as good as nonexistent in their primitive dialects. We would say: 'Don't light up'. 'I shall or I need to think this over'. Natives say: 'No lighting up'... 'Need think over'."

"Well, it looks like you've hit the nail on the head once again," the captain muttered.

39.

The day was breaking when they entered the office. Sedlintz and the other officers were having tea. They all felt cold inside, despite the 90 degrees heat. The pencil was making furrows on the paper of the police record book as each leaf in it had absorbed a lot of humidity from the air.

"Where is Director Wolfgang?" Elder enquired.

Somebody went to fetch him. The director had a hoarse voice, his hair was dishevelled, the look in his eyes weary. He was rubbing his icy hands together.

"This is terrible. This is terrible," he kept saying.

"You have little reason to complain, I should think," the chief inspector rebuked him. "But for this confounded business, you'd be poorer by a fortune. For three weeks during the most detestable season, your hotel is chock full of VIPs."

"But this scandal is terrible."

"It'll be a drop in the publicity bucket. It'll pack your hotel next season."

"My ten-year contract runs out next year, and the government will take over and run the hotel. A fat lot of good it is to me in the way of publicity."

"So you are only a lessee?"

"Yes."

"The only one?"

Wolfgang appeared hesitant.

"No," he said. "I founded the resort, and from the Malay king who was the law-abiding ruler of Little Lagonda, I got a ten-year concession for exploitation of the catering establishments. But we made it out so it's a joint undertaking, a venture on a fifty-fifty basis. The Dutch administration approved the contract, as did the contracting Neederlandische Bank."

"How is it possible to fiddle with the switchboard so easily in a hotel? From today on, a sentry shall be posted there."

"The power-house is next door to the engine-house where none but the stokers and the engine-man are ever found. We have never had any reason to take precautionary measures."

"The power-house personnel shall be interrogated. In addition, all the native people who are at present staying on the premises shall come to the office."

Wolfgang left.

"Here's the fingerprint," said Sedlintz.

"Thank you. Now take this," said Elder, and handed over a mirror that was wrapped in tissue paper. "You'll find fingerprints on this. Compare them with the one you've got."

Sedlintz buzzed off.

"Where did you get hold of this mirror?" the captain asked.

"It was last touched by the murderer's hand."

"If the fingerprints on it will match that taken from the handle, you will arrest him?"

"No. I haven't got sufficient evidence to prove his guilt."

"If it was he who plunged the whole place into darkness at the time of the assault – surely that's sufficient proof of his guilt?"

"It proves his complicity in an assault on officers of the law. However, I also want to prove him guilty of murder, blackmailing, and robbery."

"How about his alibi?"

"It's cast-iron. There'll be several reliable, bona fide witnesses who will testify under oath that they were with him at the time."

"And yet…"

"Yet he *is* the murderer."

The native personnel turned up: the men who worked in the engine house, the black lift attendant, a mulatto mixer, a Tamil chauffeur, two native scullions, the Malay vendor of picture post-cards and dance masks, and, lastly, a half-caste washerwoman.

"Ferguson, will you please take these people to the other room, and sort out those whose alibis are indisputable. I want the others to come and see me one by one."

With wide-open eyes, the coloured people stared at the policemen in fear. It was a panicky, whispering lot that followed Ferguson into the adjoining room.

"My good men," said Elder, turning to the fire-tenders in oil-stained overalls. "About an hour and a half ago, electricity was turned off in the power-house. What do you people know about that?"

"I happened to be at the hot-water boiler, sir," said the engine-man, "and I rushed out right away and, as quickly as I could, restored the power supply. Before that, a police officer, who'd come with a lamp, had been doing something there."

That was Sedlintz taking his fingerprint from the handle.

"You didn't see anybody else?"

I did see an odd type," said one of the fire tenders. "I was pushing a wheel-barrow loaded with coke from the chute, and as I came to the turning, I could see the power switchboard, For a second I spotted a man as he streaked past. I dashed after him, but lost him at the next turning. Besides I had to hurry up with the coke. He was a strange-looking sort, that guy."

"What was it you found strange about him?"

"Well, sir… I could see it quite clearly… Actually, he was a naval officer."

"What!"

"I thought it incredible, too, sir. I mean to say, a naval officer, down in the hotel basement, in the night…"

"Indeed. It is rather odd. Thank you. You people may go."

The machine-house personnel left.

Now came the turn of the natives. Only two of them were unable to produce an alibi – the washerwoman and the vendor of island curios who also sold picture postcards.

"Your name?" Elder asked the washerwoman.

"Djilda. I come from Jaipur, India."

"You are a washerwoman?"

"Yes, *sahib*. Down below. in basement. I must not come up here since *sahib* with disease has been in hotel."

"Where are your quarters?"

"In wash house. Before, I lived on upper floor, small room, but since diseased *sahib*…"

"I know about that. Did you notice anything unusual, strange last night?"

"The moon… It was red like blood… It is not so usually."

"Where did you see the moon in the basement? Can you tell me that?"

Djilda the washerwoman appeared frightened out of her wits.

"I – I dreamed…"

"Tell me no lies, woman, or I'll have your hair cropped close."

At this point the director and Martin entered. Djilda looked hard at the servant.

"If you have my hair cropped, I'll…"

"Quiet! Well, so you've come up from the basement. Why? And where did you go? Speak up or else…" And he flung up his arm, backhanded, and her knees bent beneath her in fright.

"I… I met with Martin… I love great big white servant."

"You had arranged a meeting with her?"

"Yes, sir," Martin replied hesitantly.

Elder realized that he had come to an impasse and that it was no use pumping her for more details. Yet he felt something was wrong about her.

"Get out!" he shouted at her. "From now on I'll be keeping an eye on you."

She ducked her head and quickly slunk from the room, shooting a glance of despair at Martin.

The Malay vendor of curios and picture postcards stepped forward. He was impeccably dressed in an attractive diver's suit, without the head-piece, but wearing a blue bow-tie. His black slouch hat had been stripped of its broad brim, and he wore neither shoes nor socks, but a pair of long outmoded cuffs flashed above his wrists, and he was twirling a walking-cane. A dance mask was peeping out of the pocket of his diver's suit.

"Your name?"

"Nalaya the Miraculous."

"Your trade or profession?"

"Sovereign and seller of fancy-goods."

"What?"

"I am the lord of this island, by the grace of the Queen, and joint proprietor of all catering establishments on Little Lagonda."

This piece of information came as a surprise even to Elder.

"Why, then, do you live in a squalid room, which you share with other people?"

"I do so in order to hide my identity. This sort of thing happens in great hotels at times. It's called incognito."

"And... er... Why do you sell native dance masks?"

"In order to make money."

"But you could live like a lord from your income."

"If I did, somebody else could be a seller of these things. People don't like a native manager. They like dance masks. Doing work is good. Making money is good, even if extra earnings is aplenty. It is fair this way."

He produced a mask, and admired it lovingly. Elder took it from his hand."

"Is this thing regarded as a curio on Little Lagonda?"

"It is most valuable, my dear sir, because of its rarity. So much so that it isn't even found here."

"Where does this one come from, then?"

"Leipzig, Germany. It isn't common in that city, It is manufactured there. We don't have ugly masks like this on these islands. People here have their real faces, and they're ugly enough as they are. This, too, is a great truth."

"Where were you last night?"

"I was on the floor above. I was fighting with you, and somebody fired shots after me."

"What! It was you?"

"Yes. I sneaked upstairs and went into the girl's room. I spoke with her at midnight, and when I came out, you attacked me, I got scared... Bang! Bang!... I had to run for my life."

Elder looked long into the grinning face. The explanation was either very simple or it was very clever, he thought.

"Tell me, King. Do you know who I am?"

"Everybody knows that. You are bright and old as a crocodile, and the Queen pays you for being a ruthless bloodhound, and this makes you a hated person, and they will kill you because of it."

"I see. And do you also know my customary way of treating crooks that lie to me?"

"You hit 'em and they get ill. But you mustn't hit a king."

He got a stinging smack in the face whose sound made the receptionist in the foyer wake up with a start.

"It seems to me, sir, that I was wrong. After all, you may do that," said Nalaya the Miraculous dolefully, and his eyes played him false.

"Glad we understand each other. Now you will please tell me, Nalaya, why you went hiding in a room, and why you ran away from me. But better tell the truth."

"I *am* telling you the truth. Because, you see, I very seldom tell lies. Last night somebody raised me from my sleep. It was dark, and I could not see. The old news vendor, who has a box in which dead babies' souls are crying when he turns it, will bear me witness."

"Go on."

"A voice says: 'Come downstairs, to the tool shed next to the wash-house, and you'll get plenty of money'. I had a hunch, sir, that it must be a piece of evil magic otherwise known as fishy business."

"What are you talking about?"

"Back in my days as crown prince I was a ship's stoker, and got to know civilization."

"Hm. Go on."

"It was dark in the tool shed. In there, that man, who will never turn up except after dark, in darkness, explained to me where I was to go, and that I wouldn't have to steal – I would be given some sort of copybook. When I came back he'd give me fifty florins. That's a very good offer, sir."

"He didn't tell you anything else?"

"No, he didn't, sir."

Elder ran his eye round the room.

"Is there a whip here?"

"Or rather... he said," the king went on quickly, "if I happened to come face to face with anybody, I didn't need to be afraid, as there'd be help coming... Well, after that I went back to the tool shed, and there a naval officer beat me hard because in the dark I chanced to step on his face."

"What *are* you speaking of?"

"A naval officer in a grey uniform pushed me all long the basement corridor, slapping me in the face repeatedly all the while. That's all."

"Be careful!"

"I swear by my ancestors I'm not trying to bluff, oh lightning-fisted master."

"What did he look like, the one who talked to you in whispers?"

"He was careful not to let me see him in the darkness."

"You've been telling me plenty of lies, o, King. For this, before long you'll get from me a sound thrashing that'll put you in bad health for a long, long time. This, too, is a great truth."

"But a very sad one, sir."

"Get out of here! Ferguson, go with him and question the old news vendor."

It was now Wolfgang's turn.

"What do you about what your partner just told me?"

"Nothing. His link with me is based on a very old piece of legislation. Apart from that, we have almost no dealings with each other."

Sedlintz came back.

"Here you are, sir," he said, and handed over the prints. "The two are identical beyond any doubt."

"What's that?" Wolfgang inquired.

"These are fingerprints," Elder replied with special emphasis.

The director became deathly pale, his mouth twitched in fear, and suddenly he had to sit down.

40.

Captain Dickman's uniform had become rather the worse for Felix's nocturnal wanderings. It was not before dawn that agitation in the hotel had died down sufficiently for the young man to venture to go towards the winding stairs. It was meet and proper to return the captain's apparel, he thought. For the time being, however, he was still down in the basement.

Hell! he thought as he saw that a half-caste woman and Boots were sitting at the bottom of the winding stairs. They were talking in subdued voices.

"You must believe me, Martin. That young man sent word through the head waiter that I should come... And he said to me I hadn't ironed his shirts well. He is a good-looking man, with a baby face, but for me you're the only one..."

"What did he want from you?"

"You said to me, Martin you would marry me soon as we had a thousand florins, so we can make big business... You go shine shoes in street, an' me be steam laundress."

"Speak up quick or I'll give you a couple more."

"The young man with the beautiful face said he give a thousand florins – if I help him get out of quarantine. Let him go through wash-house and at bottom of house drain, through grated door into sewage canal. It is to be at ten o'clock tomorrow night."

"Then he's the one who did the guest in."

She said gently:

"If he did that, so what?... I'm sure he needed to do that, poor thing. Some other guest will sure come along. But with thousand florins we can go to Mission an' get married."

"Hey! If they find out about this you could get as many as ten years for this."

"They no find out nothin', Martin. You will see. Young man is nice-looking and clever. Has white skin and long black eyebrows."

"He's a murderer."

"That's the sort of thing that happens at times."

"I'v got to go now. I warn you: be careful. And don't you draw me into this if there's trouble."

Felix heard a number of smacking kisses. Then Martin went upstairs, and she withdrew into the wash-house, humming a tune.

Felix started to go, too. He was about to go upstairs, to return Dickman's uniform. But what was he to put on in its stead? Farther off, close by the boiler-house, by the blue light of a safety lamp, he spotted several greasy overalls. He slipped into one of these, and put on a pair of worn-down canvas shoes he found there. There. Now he could well go upstairs.

He returned Dickman's uniform. The captain had hung it out so they would clean it. Instead, it now looked as if it had been worn out in a single night.

And now back to Maud's room.

He stole cautiously up the stairs, then slunk along the corridor. As he came to the turning, he peeked out.

He drew back in fear.

A policeman was standing guard outside Maud's room!

He instantly realised what this meant: she was under arrest. He turned and went hurriedly down the corridor. Very resolutely, and without the slightest caution, he went up to the next floor, and knocked on a door.

"Come in."

He entered. Elder, in pyjamas, was seated at the table, and was making tea.

"Did you put her under arrest?" Felix asked.

"I've only taken her into custody."

"When last night I told you all in all frankness, you promised you would ignore it."

"She volunteered to make a confession in the captain's presence. I had no choice but to detain her. Have some tea."

Felix sadly stirred the hot beverage.

"You haven't found the copybook?"

"I haven't. Those clothes were taken from the office to the laundry, and when I went to take a look, there was nothing in its pocket anymore. Someone had beaten me to it."

"Can't you find some way to help her?"

"There is some hope. I am confident."

"Look here, Elder. You and I were at school together, and we were friends. You still are my friend. Never for a moment did I harbour any ill feeling against you when you were keeping guard over me as if I'd been a prisoner, and you stole my clothes, forcing me to escape in my pyjamas. Maybe you were right to carry out my father's instructions scrupulously. I didn't bear any resentment to you. But if you will not make an exception in this girl's case, if you will prove yourself to be a stickler for the command of your duties…" He broke off. "I used to be a rather loose-living fellow," he went on. "But this is something different. I love this girl and I'm going to marry her. After she has served her sentence if she must. When she gets her release, I'll be at the prison gate, waiting for her."

"She is a splendid girl…"

"But that may not be necessary. Listen, there's nothing for it, I'll have to stay in hiding here all the time."

"I'm afraid you'll have to. You have no alibi."

"None whatsoever. It can't be helped. I'll keep on hiding. It's possible, though, that I'll make my getaway, taking her with me."

A brief pause ensued.

"Now *I* am going to tell *you* something, Felix. What you failed to mention just now is how I fared in Weltewreden. There I was, a lawyer gone broke, and you set me up with all necessities, and got me a job with the police. I will always remember that. But if you should attempt to escape with Miss Borckman, I shall be keeping my weather eye open and I'll catch both of you, and will not fail in my duty as a policeman. After that, I'll hand in my resignation – that much I owe to you as a gentleman. Both to you and to myself, since I have *you* to thank for everything I have, for what I am."

Felix rose.

"I think I can understand you."

"Do trust me and justice. Nothing has been lost yet. Have patience."

"I don't believe you."

And he left. He never took advantage of the occasion to have a shave in Elder's room, although one of his cheeks now sported a monstrously thick growth of hair. He made a beeline for the girl's room.

"What do you want?" the policeman asked, somewhat amazed to see the half-hirsute man in overalls.

"Can't I go in here?" Felix said loudly. "I have to fix the hot-water tap. We got a phone-call to come and do it."

The policeman knocked, and opened the door. Felix planted himself on the doorstep so that the girl might see him.

"Do you need a plumber, miss?" the cop asked.

"I do," she replied. "I asked for one to be sent."

"Well, buddy, you'd better snap to it," the policeman said to Felix, and stood aside to let the plumber in. Then he saluted, and again took up his post in the corridor.

When the door had been shut, Felix moved over quickly to the girl, and kissed her hand.

"Have you got the copybook?" she asked.

"It's lost. It just vanished. We haven't got much time, Maud. I'll be brief. Get your most necessary things and put them in a toilet case. Be ready to get away with me any moment."

"No."

"Be quiet!"

They spoke almost rudely to each other, and he pulled her vehemently to him, and locked her firmly in his arms.

"You will escape with me, Maud. We will go to America. Once we are out of this place, it'll be child's play to sail from any port."

"I don't want you... to make any more sacrifices on my account." She defended her stand with little enough conviction, and snuggled up against his shoulder.

"I love you, Maud. Nothing else matters. I love you, and I will share all that happens to you, whether you will get away or you won't."

Their lips almost met.

41.

When Felix re-emerged into the corridor, daytime life had started in the hotel. Guests in pyjamas and or dressing-gowns, carrying towels over their arms and soaps and tooth brushes in their hands, were heading for bathrooms – as regimented a crowd as ever graced the premises of a military barracks.

Clinking sounds came from the staircases as servants were bringing braziers they were to set up in the rooms. In several rooms, rust had begun to eat away the guests' metal objects, and mildew, which after two or three misty days is drifting in the air in the South Seas tropics, had begun to creep into ironed shirts and underwear. One intrepid merchant had asked for permission, willingly agreeing to stay in quarantine, to set up braziers at the Grand Hotel, since the establishment had no heating installations. The grate-covered containers were filled with glowing embers and placed in the rooms.

Despite the sultry weather, the "heating" was welcomed by all, as the walls had become musty, and means of protection against mosquitoes were lacking, although the heavy scent of citronella grass was suffocating.

The weather, right at the beginning of the rainy season, was unsuitable for a viable functioning of European people's organism. The plague had been isolated successfully, but there already was one case of malaria. An apoplexy-like rheumatic symptom had paralyzed Miss Jörins's legs. There were cases of aching joints, and migraine, bronchitis and gastric neurosis afflicted the hotel guests. At times the island would be enveloped in a yellowish, evil-smelling fog, that would be followed by incessant tropical rains that came in pouring down, pattering on roofs and walls, everything.

Incredible amounts of alcohol were consumed in the bar: it both kept people warm and stopped severe pains. The guests became irritable and moody. There was plenty of quarrelling and intriguing, and in one of the upper rooms a British peer shot himself in the chest. Following his suicide, it was discovered that in reality he had been a collector in the Netherlands and had been on the run because of embezzlement. In the wake of the first long-lasting downpour, there was an invasion of millions of insects and worms that came forth from the wet earth. The sprinkling of petrol practiced against the ants meant just one more distracting aroma added to the rest in the suffocating atmosphere.

Odette Dufleur, the beautiful Belgian manageress, poisoned herself with adrenalon, the drug the marquis took for his asthmatic disorders, and she was now hovering between life and death. Nobody knew about the events that had led up to the sad incident.

Several people immersed themselves in unending bouts of card-playing. Time and again the Baroness Petrovna had crying-fits, Markheit tried every possible means of calming her, and in the process lost his pocket watch.

Felix had only one wish: to be able to get a shave. He went prowling along all the corridors. At last, from one of the rooms there emerged Erich Kramartz, a young man, handsome like a film star, whose baby face was adorned by a pair of picturesquely arched, and to some extent artificially well preserved, eyebrows. He was not yet thirty. A silk handkerchief was hanging loosely from his breast-pocket; his suit, with a double-breasted jacket, was a tailoring masterpiece.

He walked away nimbly, whistling a tune.

With the master key, Felix opened Kramartz's room and entered it. He headed for the bathroom.

He whipped out the shaving things, and had just smeared his chin with the shaving cream, when the key was turned in the door.

He had come back!

Kramartz returned, in the company of Mrs Hould, an attractive, buxom lady in early middle age.

"Why do you do this, Marjorie?" he said peevishly and impatiently. "Once you've made up your mind, you'd better stop tormenting yourself."

"Oh, you must understand, Doddy. This is not so simple," she replied in a shaky voice. "Once we are out of this hotel, and Arthur has learned about everything, irrevocably, then – nothing can be done."

"But you have me."

"I do *now*. But suppose I shan't a year from now? Doddy! I have abandoned not only my husband but my children too. I have nobody but you."

"Am I not enough? I love you, Marjorie."

"You are only twenty-six, and I…"

Mrs Hould was forty-two years old, a woman with a pretty face and a buxom but well-proportioned figure. She had a few wrinkles at the corners of her eyes and about her neck, but these were only visible when she didn't apply enough powder for her make-up.

"We'll go to Cairo, Marjorie. And we will embark on a sensible venture there."

"And if we shan't succeed?"

"We will!"

"How much do you reckon you'll get for my jewels?"

"A high price. They're beautiful stones, and cut diamonds are at a premium nowadays… First thing, we'll set up a nice little nest, and we'll have enough left for us to make a living. We shall be happy, Marjorie."

"Oh Doddy. It's so difficult for me."

He threw his arms around her.

"It's because of this abominable, wet climate. It makes you feel sentimental."

"No. No. I am afraid of you. Who *are* you?"

"Are trying once again to hold against me that I was once a dancer? You despise me, maybe?"

"I'm sorry, Doddy."

"Well, I am sick and tired of this."

He opened the writing desk drawer, took from it a casket, and placed it before her.

"Here are your jewels. Take them and please return to your home."

"Don't be angry with me, Doddy. I didn't mean to hurt you."

"It's so damn humiliating, the way you keep raking up my past. I was a student reading for an engineering degree. We were reduced to poverty, my father became ill, we needed money – Well, so I went and became a dancer."

"I know, I know. Do forgive me, but… I love you and I am afraid of you. I am sorry."

He again threw his arms round her.

"My dear little, faint-hearted Marjorie. You've got to have confidence in me."

Acting with the swiftness of an old circus hand doing little acrobatic routine, Felix climbed out onto the ladder and from there down into the washerwoman's room, to re-emerge from it into the corridor. What an earth was he to do now? He would go down to the basement – there must be a quiet spot there where he would be able to have a shave.

Quickly, he made his way to the winding staircase.

The atmosphere in the basement wasn't one of peaceful calm either; workers were busy in and around the boiler-room, there was too much coming and going there. In a side-passage he spotted an open iron door.

It was the depository! The place they kept empty cases and trunks stored in. One was just being carried to the freight elevator.

"Just leave the deposit open to clear the air. And we want a brazier in there of all them trunks and cases will mildew over," Martin told the bellboy. They both entered and were gone on the elevator.

Felix stole through the door, and went far down the room. At the far end, high above the wall, was the bright patch of a small ventilation window; it gave onto the garden. There was a horrible stench in the room – he had had no idea that mouldy leather had such loathsome smell. He made for the cellar window, for he felt he was going to be sick if he couldn't get some fresh air. He pushed several trunks out of his way, and was about to shove a large trunk out of the way, but it resisted his effort. What the hell made it so heavy? He stood it up, and removed it with difficulty by turning it from one tip onto the other.

That done, he sat down on the floor and placed the razor with the mother-of-pearl handle with the name "Sydney Crick" by his side, and was rummaging about in search of the cream… He found the stench more than he could bear. He wanted to get still closer to the window. Suddenly, the top of the trunk came open, and a corpse rolled out of it and onto the floor.

It was the dead body of Mrs Villiers!

42.

Felix stood there horrified, and paralyzed with fear. The cadaver, covered with clotted blood, its mouth gaping, and with a fixed stare, its limbs crooked, lay there like a monster. In a few moments it filled the cellar with stifling stench.

He staggered towards the door, unmindful of everything in the world.

"To hell with this heap of damn mouldy trunks!" a voice sang out. "Come on, lock the depository."

The iron door slammed shut, the bolt slid home. Felix felt he might faint. He stood a large wardrobe trunk upright, clambered on top of it and from there reached the window. Not bothering about anything, he wriggled through it, and a moment later he was out in God's air. Luckily for him, nobody saw him, as out in the garden it was pouring with rain, and it was growing dusk. He ran three paces, and peered in through the next window. It was the wash-house. Just the place for him! Quickly, he jumped in.

He found a bed and a table inside – it had been furnished to accommodate Djilda for the duration of the quarantine. He saw on the table a small travelling toilet case. Had she stolen it, or had somebody forgotten about it and left it there? He sat down, exhausted and panting, and buried his head in his hands. What had happened? he asked himself.

Mrs Villiers had been murdered – a horrible gash was clearly visible across her throat. Who could have done it? Doddy, the gigolo, of course. The Sicilian widow had told the missionary how Mrs Villiers had followed Doddy here. Mrs Hould was none other than the other woman who had deserted her husband. Elder even told her name: Mrs Arthur Bocklin. Doddy was all set to make off with her jewels today. Mrs Villiers had been a serious obstacle in the way of Doddy's scheme; therefore the gigolo had done away with the editor's wife, concealed the body in a travelling chest, and simply sent it down here, to the depository. Tonight he was going to get away with Marjorie's jewels, and that would be the end of the affair.

Should he tell Elder? By no means. He, Felix, too intended to use the wash-house drain and the sewer for making his getaway with Maud. Should Doddy be caught, and if he chanced to name the spot where he had intended to escape, then they were sure to post a sentry there.

Well, let that bastard run off. After all, it was Maud who mattered.

Let that beast take to his heels and be damned!

Little by little he quieted down. He walked to the drain hole: this opening of the sewer had a grated cover and it was just large enough to allow a person to climb down the iron ladder that ran down its wall to the bottom.

First thing, he was going to have a shave, Felix thought, and went back to the table. The toilet case might contain a mirror. As he opened it he was able to establish that it had indeed had a mirror in it before, but it had either been shattered or removed. Instead, it was filled with small objects that lent themselves particularly well to being stolen from abstract-minded guests' rooms – tortoise-shell combs, sewing outfits, compacts.

He closed the small black case. Never mind, he thought, shaving wasn't an impossible feat to perform even without a mirror. He began to rummage in his pockets, for he didn't find the razor, when he heard some voices speaking.

It was back under the bed again for Felix: he did it with the polished efficiency of an escape artist. It looked as if – creeping under beds, climbing out into light-wells and hiding in wardrobes – was going to be his lot henceforward. It was no good struggling against luck like his. Possibly he had been fated for this sort of thing: perhaps his genius lay in the direction of performing such vanishing acts. In any case, by now he had grown accustomed to this sort of thing so much that a way of life that lacked any need for self-concealment in nooks and crannies might have struck him as distasteful and to be frowned upon, like something approaching exhibitionism.

Djilda entered. She was humming a tune, and placed on the floor a basket full of washing. She switched on the light, as it was growing dark.

"Hey, Djilda!" someone called. "Come here, quick!"

"What happened?"

"A dead guest has been found in the luggage depository!"

She dashed out. Martin and the bellhop had found the body when they returned to the depository with the brazier. Workers and servants, shuddering, were standing round the body.

"Don't any of you get close to it!" Martin commanded officiously. "There may be some footprints near the spot."

The black-skinned bellhop, who had gone to fetch Elder, reported, panting:

"They've arrived!"

A team of policemen consisting of the officers, Captain Vuyder, Elder and Markheit came to the scene.

"I knew it," said the chief inspector, nodding his head several times. "It's Mrs Villiers's body."

The investigation got underway. Half an hour later Corn Dealer Vangold was arrested after admitting that he was the owner of the razor with the mother-of-pearl handle bearing the inscription "Sydney Crick" that was found next to the body with the slashed throat.

43.

It was evening. In the meantime Djilda had returned to her room to resume humming her tune. She was followed by a chambermaid, who was late in coming, as she had been questioned by police. The two of them got down to putting a basketful of linen out to dry. Djilda unfolded the linen, and the chambermaid counted them.

"Two bedsheets... One pillow-case..."

"Don't count the pillow, it belongs to me... What did they question you for?"

"I was there on night duty, see? And they asked me, did I see anything suspicious on the premises. I told 'em... It's a quiet corridor, see? And Mr Vangold's a real gen'rous gent. Once he gave me a tip of one florin for taking a letter and some flowers to the Baroness Petrovna... And next day he once again gave me one florin to take to her another letter, but the baroness sent word in reply, saying no gold fountain pen had been left in her room... So he now keeps lamenting to the detective, saying he got to speak to his wife... Wants permission to speak to her on the phone."

"And what did ye tell 'em givin' evidence?"

"I said I'd seen nothing strange. I was on night duty only once... Four sheets for coverlet... The fifth's in the dressmakers' shop."

"Poor Vangold," Felix thought in his underbed hideout. He was suffering exceedingly from the ants and centipedes that were crawling all over him.

"If they'd asked you about the third floor, you'd have had quite a lot to tell 'em about, an' that's for sure. Some dirty work's afoot there, I would say. The gov'nor of Tonga Island, that Mr Shilling, an' Captain Dickman, last week they took reception of cigarettes that arrived by post for Bruns. They bribed the receptionist... Three sheets... An' I overheard by accident, an' they gave me fifty florins, they did, an' said they'd gimme another fifty if nothing of that would leak out... An' I should get the cigarettes from them an' take 'em to Bruns like they'd just arrived by post...This man Bruns, he runs arms to China, see... It's Ferdinand wot's told me that. An' that's banned under the law there, it comes in for some very stiff sentences, smugglin' arms somewhere else from Java. An' he's positively rolllin' in money, yet he was once only a sailor an' he served time too way back some years ago... Now he gets cigarettes sent to him each month from Simon Arzt, with tobacco of his own blend filled into paper with his name printed on it."

"Gee! Is that dumpy chap wot gave the lift attendant such a thrashing the other day?"

"The same. But after that, he gave him fifty florins, 'cause he ain't no bad guy, really, it's only that he's boorish and a rough customer... But now he won't give no one no thrashin' any more, 'cause he's been poisoned, an' is gonna crock, an' they'll bury him. This too is wot Ferdinand told me. He's a great one for savin' money, is Ferdinand, a very thrifty bedroom-waiter, which is why he keeps pilferin' guests' cigarettes. An' he became sick. Then he said that this man Bruns is bein' poisoned. He went right through Mr Dickman's room an' he found some sort of poison that's made from hemp an' green poppy husks, which when smoked with tobacco kills a man slowly... An' he said this called for somethin' to be done urgently, an' straight away he went an' blackmailed the cap'n an' the Britisher, an' so now he'll buy hisself a motorcycle an' side-car... You place 'm eight blue silk sheets for quilted coverlets sep'rate, dear: they belong to the private bed linen of the Belgian woman Odette. She's got everything made of blue silk, an' then she goes an' tries to kill herself. Martin says it's because the sugar tycoon wot keeps race-horses flung her over, that's why."

By now Felix was oblivious of the insects: crawling on his belly under the bed. He was aghast. He remembered how he had felt sick when smoking those "Bruns" cigarettes. Why, of course!

Those cigarettes were poisoned! And they had placed the mimosas on Bruns's doorstep – messages from Lee Shing! And this fellow was now under the impression that it was her curse that was working its pernicious effect on him.

"An' Ferdinand, when he was doin' the room, he saw that this retired chap Dickman was keepin' even brains in his drawer. An' once he overheard him sayin' to Shilling this: 'If we're permitted to enter port on Tonga Island, then the British merchant ships will go unmolested by pirates.' An' they made an agreement, but the guv'nor of Tonga Island said he wouldn't permit any loadin' of ships, and that the central guv'ment mustn't get no arms. Dickman said it was only this Bruns fellow that was supllyin' arms for them, an' so they made their pact. For this bit Ferdinand extorted from them one summer suit an' two binoculars. An' this woman Lidia, she also blackmails a lawyer from Java, 'cause he has a child bein' raised in the mission here. An' on the second floor, the lift attendant blackmails a distinguished lady on account of the Italian gen'leman rider."

"Only in the wash-house you don't get no extra earnin's ever."

Out in the corridors the lights went out, only a few small blue safety lamps were on.

"Well, good nigh'," said the chambermaid, and left, carrying the basket. Djilda switched off the light, but she didn't take off her clothes. She waited.

The rumbling of rolling wheels came from far off: they were pushing coal to the boiler. After that, silence fell, except for the loud noise made by the constant, monotonous roar of the downpour. Half an hour passed.

There came a knock at the door.

"Martin?"

There was no reply. The door was opened. Somebody entered.

"Don't switch on the light. It's me," whispered Erich Kramartz. "Open the sewer. You'll get the money when I'll be starting off. I warn you may get ten years in jail for what you are doing. So you'd better keep your mouth shut."

"Oh, *sahib*. Djilda will be mute."

Both of them were making noises as they moved in the pitch-darkness. This enabled Felix to creep out from under the bed. Kramartz was groping his way behind the washerwoman, so Felix now had an opportunity to go sneaking towards the drain hole. Kramartz was carrying a small patent-leather case. It contained Mrs Hould's jewels! the thought flashed across Felix's mind.

"It's a bit difficult to open," said Djilda, groaning as she tried to lift the grated cover of the drain hole.

"Let me do it." Kramartz went there, produced something from his pocket, struggled with the cover for a while. Then there was a clatter – and the hole was open: the sound of water streaming was heard. Kramartz snatched up the case, and handed the girl the money. The cover above him was replaced with a clash, and he hurriedly climbed down several rungs of the ladder.

Squealing and spitting, a swarm of rats scattered and scurried in all directions. He pressed closed against the wall, lest he inadvertently step into the liquid running in the sewer. The light of a small bulb was glimmering at each turning, enwrapped in steam-like reek. He had gone past the tenth way up when at last he started to climb up an iron ladder. He stopped to listen... The night was still. Thick fog lay heavy on the ground outside. Once again he produced the tool, pushed the lid up... and presently was outside!

He found himself in the natives' quarter, somewhere up the coast. A little later, at a street crossing, he heard the trotting of a rickshaw man. He clapped his hands loudly: the two-wheeled vehicle pulled up before him.

"To the harbour!" he yelled the order as he sat down. The man was off like a shot.

An hour later, he was on board the steamer bound for Surabaya. With a sigh of relief, he sank onto the narrow bed, and opened the case to take a look at the treasure it contained – Marjorie's marvellous jewels.

The case contained a diversity of small objects – tortoise shell combs, a sewing outfit, a powder compact – the sort of stuff Djilda was in the habit of purloining from hotel guests. But no jewellery.

His face pale and contorted, he let the case fall – and a multitude of gewgaws and whatnot scattered on the floor.

44.

When Djilda switched on the light, she uttered a cry in alarm. Facing her stood a half-hairy man, who was carrying a case.

"Be quiet! You have smuggled a man out of the quarantine. This will land you on Sumbava."

"I implore you, *sahib*..."

"There's only one way for you to go unpunished. I shall return here in the company of a lady in an hour and a half at the latest. She and I will descend into the sewer, and the whole business shall remain a secret. If you aren't here in an hour and a half, I will report you to the police."

"I will be here, *sahib*."

Felix mounted the stairs, carrying the small case that contained Marjorie's jewels. In the darkness, while Doddy had been fumbling with the grating, he had deftly switched the jewel case with Djilda's toilet case.

In the deserted corridor, he stopped at a door.

He listened, and heard a sepulchral voice say:

"For two days I segregated myself – but it was no use... I am lost... This was an infectious curse."

"I am sorry, Haecker," said another sepulchral vice. "I no longer detest you... You've shared my deadly solitude... Thank you... I'm grateful."

"Well, I am not."

There was the sputter of a match being struck. One of them lit up.

"You know," Bruns said in a weak voice, breathing with difficulty. "I would do a lot of things differently if... I didn't die as I must... I've been a low-down skunk and an idiot... Yet I've a lot of money... I'm rolling in it... Been positively minting the stuff... And I've never done good to anyone, never given money... for good purposes... It's too late now... Somebody has cursed me."

"I always thought this was nonsense."

"So did I... Now it's turned out to be nothing of the sort. Now, after receiving the third mimosa... I must die..."

"But what have *I* to do with it? Without any mimosas sent to me?"

"You're susceptible to curses."

He sighed heavily.

"I've done it wrong, Haecker."

"I feel giddy, Mr Bruns."

"Don't call me Bruns... My name is Hermann Thorn... But I never use this name... The police are after me... a former gangster boss... Once in Cairo, I robbed a ship's cash supply... Now I can tell anyone about it."

Silence reigned.

"Those were the days!"

Felix entered without knocking, and quickly addressed the two astonished men:

"I'll be brief," he said. "I've little time. You two gentlemen will kindly refrain from making enquiries about me. Nothing's the matter with you two. That curse business is a lot of boloney. Your cigarettes are poisoned. You must stop smoking. Drink spirits and black coffee, and in two days time you'll be all right."

"How d'you know about this?"

"Your cigarettes are being systematically poisoned by a rival gun-runner. I wish you two fellows a speedy recovery."

He buzzed off, and closed the door.

Bruns, with an astonished look in his yellowish, greasy, sweating and cavernous cheeks, stared at the door.

Then he exchanged glances with Haecker – two death's heads, for the latter, too, was in poor shape. His eyes shone weakly out of two dark holes. But he hastily picked up one bottle of brandy and pressed it against his lips.

"Those goddamn bastards," Bruns hissed. "It's those British agents that did this. But they'll be sorry for this! For if it is true that I'll get well – Well, then they're in for it... Hey, what d'you think you're doing? Put that bottle down! You aren't a goddam sponge, or something."

"Eh, what?" Haecker panted, contentedly. "Just now I thought, if you'd get well you were going to open a Sunday school:"

"Nonsense! I'll sink their bloody ships for them. Cads!... What the hell are you grinning for?"

"It just occurred to me..." he hiccupped. "By the way, why don't we go and sing us a song?"

"I won't."

"But... I make a good secretary for you."

"You are *not* my secretary and never will be."

"Reflect. Consider... Mr Hermann Thorn."

Bruns bit his lip, then said softly:

"On second thoughts, it's possible that I shall employ you."

Next day Markheit entered in his diary, in addition to the malaria patients, two cases of acute intoxication.

45.

Felix was scurrying along the corridor. He found no policeman mounting guard outside Maud's door. Was the chief inspector trying to be helpful after all? He knocked. Then he pressed down the door handle, and entered.

In the darkened room, he saw a shadow in her armchair.

"Maud," he whispered hesitantly.

"She isn't here," replied a calm voice. Elder was sitting in the armchair.

"Where *is* she,"

"In a safe place. As I knew that you were determined to escape and run off with her, I took certain measures to ensure her safety. She is being closely protected."

"Elder!"

"Look here, old chap. This is a case of justice against crime. And justice, in its cool, sober way, must triumph – in compliance with all the rules of the game. In this I believe, for this I live, and I will never compromise. She has to be cleared of suspicion. If you escape with her, you will play into the hands of a crook."

"And what if we fail to clear her?"

"Then... In that event..."

"In that event you will have ruined her life."

Elder reflected.

"Easy, Felix. We have a fair chance of success. Moreover, I'm looking for that carpet. Destroying a large Persian carpet isn't an easy job, and I don't suppose they would let the personnel in on it. They can't burn it, either. So, my dear chap, if and when the carpet is found, our case is as good as won."

"What sort of carpet is it you're talking about?"

"A rust-coloured Persian carpet."

"That's the one that Wolfgang ordered taken to Room 102 when I was taking a bath."

"What did you say? You mean that room with the caved-in wall?"

"Yes."

"Good God! I wish I'd known this sooner. Why didn't you tell me?... Come on, let's go!" Felix had never seen Elder so agitated.

They nipped along.

In the dank, musty room they found the carpet. Elder went down on his knees, and then...

Felix almost dropped with surprise: the chief inspector stretched himself out at full length, pressed his face close to the carpet – and started sniffing.

"Yes," he whispered at last. "Just as I suspected." Hi eyes shone with excitement. "You don't need to escape, old chap. Now everything's clear. The picture is complete – there's no doubt about it. Come, let's roll up the carpet."

At this moment the light went out.

"Watch out!" Elder yelled, but he was late. Someone had slipped in through the door, and gave Felix a knock over the head that laid the young man out cold. Elder fired three times – the shots reverberated formidably – but he fired into the air, not at the attacker.

There was a sudden flare as a big flame shot up from the carpet: an ether bomb had been hurled onto the carpet by someone who swiftly popped off and was out of the room. Elder didn't catch up with the person – he tripped over Felix. He pulled his friend to his feet and, dragging him along, rushed after the fugitive. However, as if at a prearranged signal, torchlights began to flash at each turning. Policemen came rushing up to take up their appointed positions. Elder ran down the iron staircase, jumping over four or five steps at a time.

The fugitive saw a torchlight flash on each floor. His pursuer was hot on his trail, and ahead of him were the police officers, one posted on each floor. He stopped in his tracks.

Elder jumped over ten steps, and hurled himself upon the man. He grabbed the fugitive by the throat, and they fell, he on top of the man.

"Someone bring a lamp here!" he yelled at the top of his voice. "Now I've got you, you blackguard! The game is up!"

"That is a great truth, sir," replied the other resignedly.

46.

The sentry that had been posted at the power-house had been knocked down.

When the switch-lever dropped, sputtering bluish sparks, and the place was plunged into darkness, a few seconds pause followed, then three shots rang out. Whoever had struck the policeman down, was off like a shot, flitted up the stairs to the mezzanine, and flitted into a room.

He stepped back, dazed, as the flash of a torchlight sprang alive, hitting him between the eyes. A police officer was covering him with a handgun.

"Stick 'em up, Wolfgang!" Sedlintz shouted. "And make it snappy!"

Before Wolfgang had time to recover from his surprise, a pair of handcuffs had been clapped round his wrists, and he was pushed into his own room. A minute later, Nalaya the Miraculous was brought in, manacled and with a bloodied nose.

Captain Vuyder was busy restoring order on the upper floor.

"Go back to your rooms, everybody," he called out in stentorian tones. "Everything's perfectly all right. Nothing to worry about."

At this, several people went off in a swoon. A police officer came racing up.

"The hotel's on fire!" he shouted.

The glass pane of the fire warning device on the wall was shattered.

Presently, the wailing sirens of fire engines were heard – the fire brigade arrived.

The Grand Hotel was ablaze! The flames leaping out of the window on the upper floor shone far and wide.

For a start, only one group of firemen passed through the quarantine, for whoever entered the hotel would not be permitted to return. Luckily, this team succeeded in extinguishing the fire, which turned out to have been a minor one, so the guests, who had been shepherded down into the foyer, were free to go back to their rooms.

Elder's prime concern was not the captives, after he had seen Felix coming along in Markheit's company. The young man was walking with a somewhat unsteady step, but at any rate on his own feet. Elder now listened to what the police officers had to report.

Previously, the chief inspector had arranged with them that, should the hotel become plunged into darkness once more, they would nip along each to his appointed post, and not budge from there, no matter what happened. He posted them to the upper floor staircases and to a number of doors.

"Where is Ferguson?"

The officer came forward. Blood was streaming down his forehead, and a long black-and-blue stain stretched across one of his cheeks.

"What happened to you?"

"I took up post… at the ground floor end of the staircase… as you told me to… Somebody came towards me… I grabbed him… and he hit me on the head."

"He can't get out of this place! We'll go right through the whole building!" Elder shouted. "Look for a man in red-chequered pyjamas. Jump to it, fellows!"

Felix went quickly to the wash-house. It was dark inside there. He had a pretty shrewd idea of the route of escape that man must have taken.

"Djilda."

"I am here, *sahib*." The light went on. The Hindu girl stood before him, trembling.

"I am looking for a man in night-clothes."

Djilda said nothing.

"If you let him go down here, tell me, and no harm will come to you. If you don't, you're in for it."

"He went down here, sir."

"What did he look like?"

"I didn't see his face, sir. It was tied up with a handkerchief."

"All right, Djilda."

The grated lid was easy to remove: it was lifted for the third time that day.

Felix descended quickly on the iron ladder and was haring away, sending lots of rusty-coloured rats scurrying every now and then.

At last, as he stopped to listen, he thought he could hear the patter of footsteps in the distance. He ran on tiptoes for all he was worth.

At one turning he spotted the fugitive. He was clad in pyjamas, and a kerchief was wrapped round his head, brigand fashion.

Presently the fugitive turned his head and saw his pursuer. He dashed on.

Felix rounded the next turning without precaution.

Two shots rang out – their reverberations in the narrow, vaulted sewer were ear-splitting.

Felix felt something hit him, and was forced to sit down close to the wall. Then everything before his eyes became blurred and dimmed out.

The man in the pyjamas with his face hidden behind a kerchief was racing on. He had covered a far longer distance than Kramartz had. He bolted up the next iron ladder. After much straining, he managed to creep out.

He found himself on pavement. Gasping for breath, he looked around.

Suddenly, soldiers and firemen closed round him.

Quickly, he snatched up his gun, but a sword, with its flat side, bore down on his hand, and the handgun dropped from his hand.

"No. That would be too simple," said Elder, coming forward from the group of men. He tore the kerchief from the man's face.

The soldiers and the firemen drew back, horrified: the captive's face was covered with unsightly red scars.

"*Mynheer* Professor Decker, I arrest you."

A pair of handcuffs clicked round the criminal's wrists.

47.

When Felix came round, he found he was lying in a hotel room, and Maud was bending over him.

"How do you feel?"

He smiled, and took her hand in his.

"All right... darling."

"You are wounded on your shoulder. The bullet didn't hit your lung. Markheit says exhaustion pulls you down more than your wound does. Here, drink some milk."

"What's news?"

"Ssh. Have some milk first." We'll talk afterwards."

But he never came round to it: no sooner had he swallowed the last gulp of milk than he dropped off again. It was late in the evening when he awoke. Maud was sitting by his side. He felt alert and healthy, and reached out to take her hand.

"Maud... I want to know how things are going with you."

She smiled. "The same old story: I am in captivity."

"Elder..."

"No," she said. "It's you. Elder says it's out of the frying pan and into the fire for me." She bent close over him. "He says you won't let me go, ever. Is that true?"

They only flew apart when the chief inspector entered.

Elder clasped Felix's hands, but his grip was firmer than usual.

"I was just speaking with your old man on the phone. I didn't mention to him that you were wounded."

"That's nice of you. I can imagine how nervous the dear old chap must have been when he saw the fire." He turned towards the girl. "Elder had sent word to my father that I am here."

"Miss Borckman, have you told him about the epilogue of the affair?"

"Felix has just awoken from his sleep. Besides, I felt it was *your* job. There is still a lot of things I can't figure out for myself."

There came a knock at the door. It was the bedroom waiter serving tea.

"Now, let me see. Just how was it?" Elder began. "Don't go to sleep over it, Ferdinand,"

"It's unnecessary for you to eavesdrop," Felix remarked. "I'll give you a summer suit and two pairs of binoculars, so don't hang around."

The waiter was stupefied, and cups clattered ever so slightly in his quivering hands.

"But I..."

"A motorcycle is out of the question. Beat it!"

Ferdinand, pale-faced, left in a hurry.

"Professor Decker is a big-time criminal," Elder began.

"What!" Felix was dumbfounded.

"You don't even know that? Decker was the phantom, the blackmailer, the crook. He made other people believe that he was Borckman."

"I felt I might go crazy when this was established with absolute certainty," she said.

"And *I* suspected this on the very first day. I too had been unaware of the initial, Russian, background of the affair until Decker told me. The professor and Miss Borckman's mother were students together in Moscow. He was in love with the pretty medical student. But then Prince Sergius appeared on the scene: he was using the name of Borckman on the basis of papers he had purchased. He and the girl fell in love with each other and got married. Decker, his vanity injured, was scouring the country in search of Borckman, He hated the man's guts. He found out that Borckman was a purchased identity, but hadn't the remotest idea that it was Prince Sergius who was hiding behind it. But years afterwards, he learned by chance that the man Borckman, whose name the prince was using, was a robber who was guilty of murder as well. His hatred and passion had never diminished over the years, so he denounced Borckman, alias Sergius, to the police. He had run the small family to earth in Achinsk. Naturally, on the basis of the denunciation against Borckman, the police would have arrested Prince Sergius. However, a friendly prefect of the police upset Decker's apple cart by giving Borckman-Sergius a chance to get away. In Shanghai, Sergius was recognized, and was thus forced to break with the Borckman family – he had become a prince once more. Decker was keeping an eye on the little family secretly, unbeknown to them. When Mrs Borckman and her two children arrived in Shanghai, he stage-managed a chance encounter, appearing before the wife as her fellow-student from the old days. Acting as their saviour, he took the woman and her children under his protection, and took them to Java. He tried hard to appear magnanimous, kind-hearted to them. I know it from him how deeply disappointed he was, for though she was grateful to him for his generosity, she had never forgotten Prince Sergius. However, she trusted her former colleague unquestioningly, and revealed to him the secret: that her husband was not Borckman, but Prince Sergius. The doctor – for at that time Decker was not yet a professor – had found a more realistic goal than his wild-goose chase. For a few weeks he left for Paris, and started to blackmail the prince, pretending to be the 'real' Borckman. From the extorted money, he set up his first laboratory on Java; from the money he had extorted, he was generous to the Borckman family. He had begun to lead his Jekyll-and-Hyde life. Whenever he left for a few weeks, the serious professor would live in grand style in Tahiti or Hawaii. He owned a villa and a yacht, kept a mistress, and would take part in every game and gambling from stock exchange to roulette. After these flings, he would return to Java, where as a serious scientists he carried on truly valuable work. Eventually, with his banana oxide he achieved his highest accomplishment: it was purchased by the government for five hundred thousand Dutch florins.

"Huge losses incurred on the stock exchange and his extravagant double life raised the threatening prospect of total ruination. This five hundred thousand florins was just enough to iron out difficulties and avert disaster. And now he sought to raise another five hundred thousand florins. He knew of a state that was prepared to pay five hundred thousand to be able to recover the sole right of sale from Dutch hands. But the illustrious professor would have had to sacrifice his position and status if he had stolen his own invention. So the plan was conceived: he would use blackmail in order to force his secretary, Maud, to steal the notes on the Banana Oxide, and make her escape. Her private secretary being on the run would have put the professor above suspicion, and left no doubt as to the identity of the guilty person. The rest happened here. Miss Borckman had no choice but to remove the notes. She believed that she was defrauding her boss for the benefit of Borckman. She was unaware that the two were one and the same person. Following Borckman's instruction, she came here, to the Grand Hotel, and a getaway airplane had been got ready to help her continue her escape. Decker used the pretext of attending a congress to be nowhere near by at the time of the theft. He had shaved off his beard, and came here incognito, and took an inexpensive room on the ground floor. Then, during the night, one way or other, he would have got hold of the copybook, posing as Borckman, but in a way that he would not have been brought face to face with Miss Borckman."

"He was due to pick it up from her doorstep," Felix said.

"Fortunately, at this point the drama turned into tragicomedy. Two con men – Wolfgang and his crony, a native tribal chief, Nalaya the Miraculously Brazen-Faced – ten years ago told a pack of lies about Little Lagonda that was sufficient to get it developed into a bathing resort. The native ruler and Wolfgang secured for themselves a franchise on all catering establishments here for a ten-year term. This ten-year term has now run out. Next year the bank will take over the running of these businesses. The two con men were bent on making the most of this last opportunity. To this end they had a brainwave: extend the season by three weeks at a time of year when as a rule not a single guest comes here. This, computed in terms of eighty guests, means a turnover of over a hundred thousand florins – and they would have cleaned out the till all right, I'm sure. But how could one lengthen the season? By having quarantine imposed on the place. That lasts exactly for three weeks. Nalaya knew a vegetable poison that brings on symptoms typical of bubonic plague but otherwise causes no deadly complications. They selected an unimportant guest in order to poison him a little for the good cause. They were misled by Professor Decker's unassuming incognito. There was only one bedroom waiter to be let in on the matter – he had the job of slipping the poison into the professor's coffee. They paid that man fifty florins. Stinginess has proved the ruin of many a crook, and that is what happened in this case. The waiter took in the coffee to Decker, and the professor became unwell by next morning. Now came Dr Ranke. The doctor was a greedy, incorrect man. He just took a look at the professor, and asked two questions, and it was clear to him that there was a case of bubonic plague. After that, he handed him, from a safe distance, the conventional medicament – Palmyra oil – so that the patient would be able to rub it on his body. This got the professor wised up to the nature of his illness. The oil with the stuffy smell alleviates the terrible burning feeling caused by the festering plague sores. As he was applying the oil, he asked the doctor, who was standing on his doorstep, straight out:

'Dear Colleague. I am Professor Decker, incognito. It is absolutely necessary that I know the truth: Have I contracted bubonic plague?'

"The doctor was absolutely candid. 'Yes, professor,' he said. 'It is a typical case.'

"At best one out of ten thousand people infected with bubonic plague is cured of the disease, and even he will remain a pitiful wreck for the rest of his life. So Decker decided that he should release the victims he had ensnared. He asked Dr Ranke to settle the affair. He should go upstairs to Room 88 (At the time Maud was still the occupant of Room 88, only the day after did she exchange rooms with Lindner.) He was to tell Miss Borckman that she could take the invaluable notes back, return them, and live in peace thereafter. He, Decker, had been posing as Borckman. Ranke caught on at once: he knew this was a tremendous opportunity offering itself: a once-in-a-lifetime chance. He was alive to the importance of the Banana Oxide. So he did not report the plague case immediately; instead, he asked Maud for an appointment during the night. That was when you crept in through the window, wearing pyjamas."

"At least now I know where she had been," said Felix, and took her other hand as well.

"Ranke went to the meeting, pretending to be in the know about the whole affair, and cleverly wormed the gist of it out of her. After that, he blackmailed her, and demanded that the copybook be handed over to him. He gave her until the following day. Next morning Wolfgang and the native learned from Ranke who the alleged 'travelling salesman' was. But the culpable bedroom waiter found it out, too. He realized that he had been made to run the risk of being sentenced to life-long imprisonment for the paltry sum of fifty florins! While the doctor was reporting the case on the telephone, this waiter went in to the patient. Decker had begun to have suspicions about a case of bubonic plague that was without high temperature and symptoms of paralysis. The waiter, to save his skin, spilled the whole thing about the poisoning to the patient. Decker at once sized up the situation. He gave the waiter money to seal his mouth. He could hardly wait for Dr Ranke to come back. In the meantime the police committee had arrived, and imposed the quarantine. No sooner had Markheit left the doorstep of the sick room than Decker slunk up the stairs. Meanwhile, Dr Ranke hurried to Room 88, but he found Lindner in occupancy there, as he had switched rooms with Maud. He asked for Lindner's permission to use his telephone. Lindner left the room, as the police had called upon all guests to go down into the foyer. Ranke had just picked up the receiver, and was about to ring Maud when the patient showed up. Words passed between them, and the row led to them grappling on the floor. This could be seen from the dead man's torn-off necktie and torn shirt. Flooring the poisoned sick man was a pushover for Ranke, but before he could have left the room, Decker snatched up the stage dagger, which was lying on the writing desk, and stabbed the doctor to death. Following this, a lot of people in a state of hysteria made their appearance on the scene. *Signora* Relli lugged the dead man from Lindner's room. Maud, believing it was the prince who had committed the murder, concealed the dagger. The strange noise lured Felix to slink over to investigate, and as he feared he might fall under suspicion, dashed back to his hiding-place, but he had lost a button from his pyjama and it was found by the side of the corpse. All these occurrences seriously hindered the investigation. Luckily, however, I found an important clue: I recognized on the corpse a quite mild, but nevertheless unmistakable, smell of oil – a little had rubbed off from Decker onto it. So it happened that I followed up the right clue. The scuffle had left its marks upon the body, but no trace of it could be found in the room. Whatever blood stains were found there, too, were too little compared to the size of the wound. So I came to the assumption that the carpet which they had fought on and which blood had run onto, had disappeared. I was sure that the smell of Palmyra oil must have been preserved on that carpet, too. But Decker thought of that also. Wolfgang and the native were under his thumb. If Decker was caught, and the poisoning, the faked plague, came to light, it meant terribly stiff sentences for them. The professor took advantage of the two entrapped men – they became his slaves. Wolfgang made the carpet disappear, and Nalaya carried the letter. Once, in the darkness, Wolfgang even knocked me down. The nurse was sound asleep, the doctor would only visit him by day – on these occasions Decker would simulate illness. However, we managed to secure a pocket mirror bearing the professor's fingerprint and get it out of the sick room, and this matched the fingerprint that was taken form the power-house switchboard handle. We made thoroughgoing preparations for the third blackout. Ferguson, obeying my instructions, dashed to the staircase that blocked the sick-room. Decker could not get back, and was forced to flee."

"How did you people catch him?"

"Markheit had considered the quarantine to be lifted before the fire broke out, because Wolfgang's confession had made it clear that there was no real case of bubonic plague in the building. I hurried after you, as I had been keeping an eye on you – after all, I had assumed responsibility for you. Djilda sang as soon as I threatened her. I packed the fire engine with soldiers, and we drove all along the sewer, with three men taking up positions at each manhole. We got to the last but one manhole at the same time as Decker, and there we collared him."

"How about Mrs Villiers?"

"Accidentally, a totally separate crime also took place at the hotel. The jealous woman threatened the gigolo. Years ago, the two of them were a pair of dancers known as 'Doddy and Amy'. This time Doddy was out to pluck another woman, clean her out of her jewels, and when Mrs Villiers had become a danger to him, he removed her, dispatched her. A warrant is out already for his apprehension. All the culprits involved have made admissions. Decker has asked me not to have the Borckman case entered on record. I did grant him his request – with much pleasure."

"Thank you," Maud whispered.

"Elder, old chap, you're great!"

"Great is truth, and mighty above all things," replied the chief inspector.

48.

An exodus started from the Grand Hotel to the ship. The Baroness Petrovna and Miss Jöring made a voyage together to the Javanese hills. Lindner and Signora Relli were preparing to return to Italy where they would get married. Haecker, in his capacity as private secretary to Mr Bruns, booked two seats on a flight to Shanghai. Both of them were as fit as a pair of fiddles. The rooms had been vacated, and the staff were looking into nooks and crannies in a hunt after belongings the departing guests might have left behind. An ambulance took Odette Defleur to a sanatorium. And it was raining in torrents.

The whining lament of a barrel-organ came from under the glass portal of the hotel.

Marjorie had grown old overnight. Doddy had vanished – along with her jewels. It was all right for her to return home – after all, she did have an alibi: she had been Signora Relli's guest. But what could she tell Arthur about the jewels? No, she felt she couldn't possibly go home like this. Where was she to go, then?

She cast a glance at the cheerless, bottle-green water. Several large birds were flying under a blind sky.

Yes, there was no other way.

"Excuse me, ma'am." A servant stopped her in the vestibule. "You have left this in the room, ma'am," he said, and handed to her – her jewel case!

Marjorie opened it... She touched her hair... There they were... All of her jewels were in the case.

Had she gone crazy? Was this possible?

"Who are you?" she asked, gasping for breath.

"A servant, ma'am. The Servant of Destiny. For this once, ma'am. But this is the last time. You understand, don't you? Have regard for your husband, and rejoice in your children. *Au revoir*."

The Servant of Destiny vanished out of her sight – and made his way to Elder.

"How lucky, old chap," he said, "that you found the jewels in Maud's room, I'd forgotten about them completely, yet they may have saved this woman's life."

"Come on," Elder said. "Your old man's been playing host to Prince Sergius and Maud for two hours. I hope this time you're not going to hook it in your pyjamas to give the slip to the church bells."

"Not likely."

They started off, but Felix stopped.

"Tell me... About that dagger I threw out of the window. How come it turned up?"

"It was in one of Captain Vuyder's boots."

"Where?... Who put it there?"

"I did. I wouldn't have him to arrest Vangold. So, after I'd found the dagger in the garden, I slipped it into our good old captain's boot. I hope to God he won't find out about it."

"And what about the copybook with the banana oxide?"

"It's already in the possession of the authorities concerned. I found it in the manager's office, in the inner pocket of the bellhop's jacket. Just as you said."

"And you denied it to my face!"

"Sure. If I didn't, they would have given it up to Decker. Come on, let's go."

In the governor's villa, a group of happy people was sitting around the dinner table. Outside, it was pouring with rain, but none of those present seemed to mind or care a damn. The governor was happy to have his son back, Elder was happy about his promotion, and Felix was happy about everything, for under the table cover he was clutching Maud's hand all the time.

A news item:

The Alcazar nightclub in Singapore was the scene of a strange drama. A jealous female dancer shot to death Erich Kramartz, who under the stage-name of Doddy featured on the programme as an acrobat-dancer. Kramartz died on the spot...

By the time the curtain was rung down, in the shape of a shroud, over the last scene of the drama, Little Lagonda was firmly locked in the embrace of thick, evil-smelling, muggy fog.

A newly-wed couple arrived in Hawaii on their honeymoon.